Simmer Down, Mr. C

Simmer Down, Mr. C

a novel

Scott Bitely

AMBASSADOR INTERNATIONAL
GREENVILLE, SOUTH CAROLINA & BELFAST, NORTHERN IRELAND

www.ambassador-international.com

SIMMER DOWN, MR. C

This is a fictional work. Names, characters, places and incidents either are the product of the author's imagination or are used fictitiously. Any resemblance to actual persons, living or dead, events or locations is entirely coincidental.

© 2012 by Scott Bitely

ISBN: 978-1-62020-104-6
eISBN: 978-1-62020-157-2

Cover design and typesetting: Matthew Mulder
E-book conversion: Anna Riebe

AMBASSADOR INTERNATIONAL
Emerald House
427 Wade Hampton Blvd.
Greenville, SC 29609, USA
www.ambassador-international.com

AMBASSADOR BOOKS
The Mount
2 Woodstock Link
Belfast, BT6 8DD, Northern Ireland, UK
www.ambassador-international.com

The colophon is a trademark of Ambassador

THIS BOOK IS DEDICATED TO THOSE WHO
UNDERSTAND THAT THE TRUE MEASURE OF
SUCCESS IS NOT FOUND IN A TEST SCORE.

Contents

Plans fail for lack of counsel,
but with many advisers they succeed.

~ Solomon

CHAPTER I

Almost Ready

I'm blaming it on Hollywood. The reason I went into teaching, that is. They made it look so easy. The sitcoms and dramas on television always showed really cool and attractive teachers in blue jeans and sport coats (complete with velvety patches on the elbows) who lectured their classes with noble thoughts and ideas. With the exception of maybe a handful of individuals, the students on TV always appeared to be in-tune with the teacher's flow of instruction. Any disagreements or variations from the instructor's plans were dealt with quickly and efficiently. (If Zack Morris was as bad as it got on *Saved by the Bell*, the teachers at Bayside had it pretty good.) Anything witty or slightly humorous was met by two to three seconds of laughter. Nothing more. And if for some strange reason the class started getting too restless, the bell always rang.

But I never imagined someday I'd be teaching sixth grade, let alone in the *exact* same room in which I was held captive some twelve years earlier. Walking into Room Five again, almost a dozen years after spending an entire year in this room, was somewhat strange. For a moment, I thought of Ms. Horter welcoming me on that first day of school so many years ago. I remember the way she hugged me. Thankfully it was a side-to-side hug, not straight on. The overwhelming smell of perfume and baby powder radiated in sharp, penetrating waves. To this day, when I smell talcum powder, it takes me right back to this place. I remember being very nervous. The kind of nervous where the contents of your stomach can't decide which way to go.

As I stood there looking at my *new* classroom, that same feeling began to creep slowly into the pit of my stomach. Looking around, I had no idea where to even start. The room was a throwback to the 1950s or early 60s because the taxpayers of Coleman hadn't passed a millage in decades. Much of the materials in the room looked very familiar. As a student, most of the stuff seemed old. Now, it all looked ancient. The only thing I knew for sure was that I had a lot of work ahead of me. School started in six days.

I'd graduated from college in the spring and sent out resumes all over the state with the vigor of a beggar looking for loose change. The only place not on my list was Coleman Public Schools—in my hometown. I'd interviewed twice during the early summer months in neighboring districts. Neither went well. Looking back, it wasn't hard to figure out why. During the first interview, when asked why I went into teaching, I drew a blank. The only thing coming to mind was "June, July, and August." My Uncle Byron was a woodshop teacher, and I distinctly remember hearing him say that phrase all the time. He didn't like kids, and apparently that's the message I had sent the interviewers as well.

They'd also asked me what I'd do if I were to catch a student cheating. My lack of confidence, combined with uncertainty concerning the kind of an answer they were looking for, caused me to ramble on for quite some time. I ended by saying, "I mean…we've all cheated at some point in time, haven't we?" My rhetorical question was met by sheer mystification on behalf of my interrogators. Suddenly, they seemed in a hurry to finish the interview, never a positive sign.

The second interview wasn't much better. I told them what I thought they wanted to hear, but they went with the secretary's son-in-law instead.

As the summer wore on, the tension began to rise. Going back to Larry's Lumber, the place where I'd worked during the summer months in high school, was not even on the radar. Some of my friends were still there, doing the same thing year after year. Not for me. While in college, I managed to land a job at Gretchen's Irish Pub to earn money that was directly applied towards rent and tuition. It was hard enough working there to help pay for school, but to work there as a college graduate would be tough to swallow. I could already imagine the conversations I'd have with some of the patrons. "You know," someone with a little too much booze in his bloodstream would say, "you could have saved yourself a few thousand dollars and just stayed here and worked for the last four years instead of a-goin' to that there college." So I did everything I could to land a teaching job. By the middle of August, the desperation inside caused me to grow extremely anxious, as it appeared there were no possibilities.

With the beginning of a new school year inching closer, I found myself one day in the middle of the afternoon at Gretchen's. I hadn't decided if I was going to ask her for a job or drown my sorrows. Perhaps a drink first and then I'd check if she had an opening. Gretchen was well under five feet tall, weighed about 85 pounds, and she sure as shootin' wasn't Irish. Her last name is Heinderich. German. It wasn't uncommon to see her throw men three times her size out the front door—not one to put up with any junk. No one's really sure why it's called Gretchen's Irish Pub. Maybe she just liked the name.

"What'll it be, Teddy?" she asked as I approached the bar. She was cleaning shot glasses.

"What's on tap?" I asked.

"The same thing that's been on tap for the last twenty-two years," came her smart-aleck reply.

"How about a Coke," I responded.

"Coming up," she said. "So tell me. What brings you around?"

"Well, I have absolutely nothing to do. Just finished watching *General Hospital*, and I'm waiting to hear from a school in Carleton about a fourth grade teaching position."

"Have you checked with Carol up at the school?" Gretchen asked. "If I'm not mistaken, there's a sixth grade opening. You ought to look into it."

"No, I don't think I want go back there."

"Why not?"

"Oh...I don't know. Seems like it would be a little awkward going back there to teach."

"Why's that?" she wondered.

"I don't know. It just seems like it would be kind of weird teaching right alongside some of my former teachers. I didn't exactly have the best relationship with some of them."

"You know," she said, "that's about the dumbest thing I've ever heard. You think you're too good to stay in Coleman and teach?"

"Well, no... not really," I replied, although my tone said otherwise.

"Is that right? I can see right through you, Teddy. I've known you way too long to know that you're talking a bunch of horsepucky, mister." Like I said, she didn't put up with any garbage. Besides my grandma, she's the only one allowed to call me Teddy. Born Eugene Theodore Carter, it was through a series of strange and confused looks that my parents decided to call me Ted. Eugene simply wasn't going to cut it. It's very difficult for a lad of seven or eight to go around with a name more commonly associated with old men. Having people call me Theodore wasn't any better, so by default, they called me Ted.

"I'll think about," I said, referring to the sixth-grade position. Beggars can't be choosers. However, the last thing I wanted was to end up living at home with my parents, teaching in my hometown.

———

Taking Gretchen's suggestion, I dropped off a resumé. I was a little panicky with the thought of student loans hovering over my head for the next several years. When Don Boggins, the principal of the kindergarten through eighth grade building in town, called to set up an interview with the start of school just a few weeks away, I felt some relief. To my wonder and amazement, he called back a few days later and offered me the job. With no other possibilities on the horizon, I accepted his offer.

The relief at having a job was short lived. I quickly realized the real work was about to begin, as there's a lot more that goes into being fully prepared than just showing up a few minutes before the kids.

The six days preceding the start of school were extremely busy. I felt like an over-caffeinated gerbil rushing from one task to another. There was an incredible amount of work that needed to be done to get this class ready. Despite the fact that I was crossing things off my to-do list, I wasn't gaining much ground. For every item removed, there were two or three other things that needed doing that weren't even on the list.

Rummaging through supplies and materials, I noticed a reoccurring theme. Everything was old and outdated. Looking at the students' desks, I remembered exactly where I sat when I was in Ms. Horter's class. Right behind Becky Daniels. She was beautiful. So many times Ms. Horter's voice became only a small vibration in the background as I envisioned rescuing Becky from a horrendous, catastrophic event. Of course, she and I would be the only survivors. The continuation of the species was up to us, and I was more than happy to take on that responsibility. She would be injured somewhat, but not so much that it changed her appearance. Maybe I would have to carry her on my back for several miles because her leg was cut and bleeding and she couldn't walk on her own. Taking off my t-shirt to use as a tourniquet, she'd see my tanned chisledness. My huge, rippling muscles would be sure to raise her blood pressure…in a good way. She'd tell me how glad she was that it was just the two of us and how secretly she, too, wished something like this would happen. My dream always came to a screeching halt as either I'd hear Ms. Horter's voice calling my name and demanding a response to a question I hadn't heard or Becky insisting I get my legs out from under her seat because she didn't want to *accidentally* touch me. She obviously didn't feel the same.

Standing there in the quiet, it wasn't hard to imagine hearing Ms. Horter's voice again. "Simmer down, class," she said, always followed by "Simmer. Simmer." With exactly two seconds between each *simmer*. We timed her. It got to a point where half the class would mouth the word *simmer* as she was saying it. Being that I was in the sixth grade, and with the onset of adolescence, everything was funny. My friends and I would break out laughing whenever we had a chance to say, "Simmer. Simmer." We could be playing football, or whatever, and if things got a little heated, all one of us had to do was say, "Simmer. Simmer." and we'd bust a gut and forget about whatever impending infraction had caused tempers to flare in the first place. For a brief moment, I wondered if the students coming my way would find anything funny in my mannerisms.

Standing in the middle of my classroom, looking out at a sea of desks, the shelves lined with countless textbooks, I had no idea where to even begin.

CHAPTER 2

Home

C oleman is nestled between the hills of U.S. 131 and M-34 in northern Michigan. To most who have made their home here, it's a small slice of paradise where the real beauty lies not so much in the middle of town, but rather on the gravel roads and two tracks that connect our town to others. Rolling hills, fertile farmland, and just enough people and businesses to keep things balanced. For those wanting to get out (most of the town's adolescent population), it's a barren wasteland of dead-end hopes and dreams. Their greatest fear is that they'll end up just like their parents. To them, their parents shine as living examples of people who settled for a lot less than they once hoped.

The only sight that let you know it wasn't still 1947 in Coleman were the vehicles parked along the streets. Apparently, the village budget for beautification and improvement was very small—or nonexistent.

We don't believe in excess. One of everything suits folks just fine. Having two grocery stores would only cause problems for people who don't like to make tough decisions. When the flier for Glen's Supermarket comes tucked inside the Public Pulse, our town's newspaper, people don't even give a second thought to going anywhere else. It doesn't matter that they can drive into Hollisford a few miles away and save twenty-seven cents on a gallon of milk at one of those *Get-everything-you-need-and-then-some* stores. People know Glen, and that's what makes the difference. The fact that he actually answers your questions himself instead of sending you to another person in the store (who oftentimes would offer less help than the person doing the sending) offers a certain element of security.

Next to Glen's is Moore's Hardware Store. Now into its third generation, Pete Moore offers something those big million-square-foot national chains can't. Pete greets you by name when you enter the big glass double doors, and he usually knows what you need before you ask. Sure, the prices are a little higher than the *big guys*, but it's a small sacrifice most are willing to make. Pete once told me, "As long as the lights are on, we're open." Meaning the hours posted out front were only an approximation.

The Taste-T-Freeze, owned by Harold Dennison, is a few doors down from Moore's and has been keeping customers fairly happy every April through September since 1956. With the exception of the prices, nothing has changed on the faded, oversized display picturing sundaes and banana splits. Varying the selections or offering more items would only cause Harold and his workers inconvenience as they waited for people to make up their minds. Harold's a great guy, but definitely one to avoid aggravating. His patience had not increased with age. Experience had taught us that he would sometimes *forget* to fill our order to its anticipated size if he detected even the slightest tone of impertinence. It was fun to watch people from out of town learn this lesson. Standing behind them in line, concealing our giddiness, we occasionally watched offending customers walk away from the sliding window holding their vastly under-scooped cones. Their faces revealing varying degrees of confusion, anger, and just a tinge of regret.

As a Little Leaguer, my baseball coach would take us to the Taste-T-Freeze twice each season. Win or lose. Coach always said, "Get whatever you want." Then he'd wait a few a seconds and add, "As long as you keep it under fifty cents." Which basically meant you could get a small soft serve ice cream cone.

No sprinkles. Not dipped in chocolate sauce that hardened to a sweet, chocolaty shell. Just plain. Kind of like us.

The Coleman Community Church is just a short walk from most of the small businesses downtown. The large brick building, surrounded by massive oak trees, was a place I used to visit often with my grandma and grandpa when I was younger. At this point in my life, sleeping in seemed a lot more attractive than sitting in a hard pew for an hour.

If you were to stand on the outskirts of town just past the railroad tracks and observe, you'd notice that Coleman is similar to other small Midwestern towns. There's the Pere Marquette Railroad running north and south on the eastern edge of town directly across from Roy's Barber Shop. The grain elevator is, of course, right next to the railroad tracks. A four-way stop with its red blinking light in the middle of downtown is all that's needed to keep motorists in line.

Most families making up this town have been here for years. There aren't a lot of new people moving in to take up residence, and that's the way we like it. Sure, there are occasional families who move in, but mostly those in transition. They might stay for a short while, but when their relationship status changes, or a better offer comes along, they leave, which explains why the population has hovered around fifteen hundred for much of the last sixty years.

To those living in surrounding towns, there's mostly a sense of satisfaction that they *don't* live here. Who'd want to live in a place where things never change? A place where you recognize someone a half mile away, not because of your extraordinary eyesight, but because you can make out their blue pick-up truck with the rust spots resembling an appaloosa. Of course, there are also those families who were fairly easy to spot from great distances simply because of the shape and size of their heads.

It's a one-newspaper kind of town. The Public Pulse shows up in the press box every Tuesday morning (along with the flier for Glen's). There was quite a stir several years ago when the printer forgot the *l* in Public, raising a few eyebrows. Most people thought it was pretty funny, though a few of the conservative folks were none too pleased.

In the muggy summer months, it's not uncommon to hear older folks saying things like "It's not so much the heat as the humidity that's driving me crazy." During the winter, older gentlemen say things like "Well, I guess they're saying it's supposed to get cold." Weather in the Midwest has long been *the* topic to break awkward silences that seemingly pop up between people.

A lot of these same guys gather at The Oak Floor Inn, owned by Jim and Pam Wilson, every morning for breakfast. The heavy smell of grease accumulating on their attire makes it easy to tell who's been to The Oak Floor and who hasn't. They don't usually eat a whole lot, mostly sit around the table and consume large quantities of coffee and complain about the cost of a gallon of gas. Guys say things like "I seen a bunch a deer this morning out behind the barn at the ol' Smith Place when I brang my tractor to Clarence's to have him fix 'er" or "Did you guys know you can get your truck warshed for free with a fill-up of twelve gallons or more of premium gasoline at The BP? I don't know how they stay in business doin' that."

Every now and again, one of these guys will order Jim's famous meat and cheese omelet. It only has three eggs, but the tremendous amount of bacon, sausage, ham, and cheese cause it to drape over the sides of the plate like a greasy, slimy tarp. The vertical distance is comparable to a coffee cup. It's not called "The Binder" for nothing. Sure, a guy could probably go several hours without having to eat again, but the after-effects of consuming that much meat and cheese have a way of causing a little traffic jam in the lower intestinal tract.

These old guys always take advantage of the smallest opportunity to drive into town. A seven cent bolt at Moore's Hardware (and sometimes a "warsher" to go with it) is enough of a reason. These were the kind of guys that liked to sit around the *Topper's Table* at The Oak Floor and try to impress each other with the amount of rain in their rain gauges. "Got sixth- tenths this morning," one would say. Of course, the unwritten rule is that unless there's more rain in your gauge, you keep your mouth shut. "Yeah, we got almost an inch in our gauge," someone else would reply. The first one to bring up the topic never stood a chance, hence the name Topper's Table. During the summer, the competition centered around the heat, and in the winter, the cold. In addition to being the kind of guys who defined their manhood by the truck they drove, they were also the kind of guys who quite often referred to their wife as *mother, ma, the ol' lady, the wife, the warden,* or even *the ol' ball and chain*...never in her presence, though.

The location of Coleman has us receiving only a handful of radio stations, the majority of which play country music. Due to the fact that Coleman is at the bottom of a large valley, reception is limited to clear, sunny days. On rare occasions, we could pick up a heavy-metal station broadcasting from downstate, WKIL, whose heavy rotation of Black Sabbath and AC/DC made them barely palatable.

Like most towns, we have a few local celebrities too. Our most famous resident, Todd Szepanski, played one year of baseball at the junior college level. He now coaches the JV team at the high school. Has for seventeen years. When he's not on the diamond reminding the kids how great he used to be, he shares duties with his identical twin brother, Tom, driving a tow truck. Baseball practice consists primarily of Todd launching fly balls toward the center field fence while his players run around the outfield trying to shag his line drives. His philosophy: Kids are more apt to listen when they're in awe of the coach.

Another local celebrity, Carol Carroll, is the school secretary for the K-8 building in town. Her prominent status hinges primarily on her name. For twenty and one-half years, she was known around town as Carol Smartz, but she found herself unable to resist the temptation that was Robert Carroll, the tall, lanky son of a pig farmer who lived about a half mile up the road from her parents. With a name like that, combined with a position in public service, everyone knows her.

Neighboring towns always seemed so glamorous and mystifying when I was younger. To some extent, they still do. Fifteen minutes east of Coleman is Hollisford. Those high-class, latte drinking snobs reminded us all the time of our subservient status by their haughty demeanor. Their eyes full of contempt and disgust. There was something else in their eyes as well. Gratitude. An appreciation that they didn't have to go through life like us. We were the poor farming town; they were the wealthy white-collar crowd. While we were stuck living on roads with names like Sixteen Mile or County Road 408, they were making their homes on streets with names like Maple Ridge Vista and Pine Valley Way. As a child, I envied their cushy lifestyle, but never their character.

Having Hollisford so close did provide an education I wouldn't have gotten anywhere else. The kids in Hollisford were the first ones to help me understand the different kinds of tough. When it came to sports, they were tough. After thrashing us in football, it always amazed me that no one on their team was limping or holding an arm or neck or any other place that hurt. They beat us up on a regular basis. We could always hear them long before their bus pulled into the school parking lot. Having sixty boys stick their heads out of the bus windows and *moo* can make quite a racket.

As they boarded the bus and headed home to celebrate another victory, a lot of my teammates were on their way home to get some rest, as many of them would be up at the crack of dawn helping their fathers or uncles in the fields or barns or wherever work needed doing. Waking up at 4:30 a.m. to shovel cow manure or rake a field of hay never helped us score touchdowns, but it did instill an appreciation for hard work. The calluses on our hands were worn as badges of honor. Half the guys I played football with smelled like cow pies. We were tough too. It was just a different kind of tough. The kind that doesn't win football games.

While the kids in Hollisford were sleeping off the party from the night before, most of us had been up for several hours with not so much as a fleeting thought to last night's game.

Another reason I was sometimes envious of kids from other towns was because of our school nickname and colors. Because the name of our town was synonymous with camping gear, someone along the line decided we would be known as the Screamin' Lanterns. Prior to 1971, we were the Coleman Comets, but with the ever increasing sales of coolers, sleeping bags, and of course lanterns, the school board thought a name change necessary. The Coleman Screamin' Lanterns. Enough to put us in the weird category, but certainly not enough to instill fear and trepidation in our opponents, especially when our mascot showed up at games. It's difficult to make a lantern look terrifying and vicious. And while we all would have preferred dark green and white, that was not to be. Lime green and white defined us.

There was a stretch in the late 1980s and early 1990s when our basketball team won two games over a seven-year stretch. We landed in the record books for the most consecutive losses. Fifty-two straight. Attendance increased somewhat as folks had to see what all the hubbub was about.

When your parents went to school with everyone else's parents, it creates a climate of familiarity. Sure, we don't know each other *that* well, but we know each other well enough. When I was eight years old, I spent the night at Darryl Clippenstein's house. (We called him Clip to make it easier on everybody—including him.) His dad caught us using a screwdriver to carve our initials onto the side of his new riding lawn mower. It wasn't brand new, but it was new to him. He took it upon himself to give us both a spanking. My parents were aware of the situation but never said a word to me. They figured Darryl's dad had handled it. That's how close-knit our town is. A place where a guy can give some other kid a beating and have nothing come of it.

Clip was my best friend growing up. We were inseparable throughout our entire K-12 education. We were such good friends that our voices actually started cracking within two days of each other. That wasn't a coincidence. I'm sure it had something to do with the fact we were around each other so much. Sometimes we were lucky enough to end up in the same classroom. After seventh grade, most of the teachers were wise enough to place the two of us in a different class. We got busted in middle school choir more than once for adding "under the sheets" to every song Mrs. Buckley announced. She'd say, "All right, class, turn in your songbooks to page sixty-five; we're going to sing 'It's a Small World.'" Then we'd mumble our phrase just loud enough for those around to hear. If we hadn't been moved to the front row for an earlier offense, we probably could have gotten away with it. Our favorite song for her to announce was "Hot Cross Buns." It didn't really even make sense to say "under the sheets," but we just about died laughing every time. Middle school boys need very little ammunition to act like complete idiots. Mrs. Buckley got the last laugh, though. Walking into class one day, she quietly informed me I would be in wood shop for the rest of the semester.

My family consists of my mom and dad and my brother Thad. Short for Thaddeus. He used to punch me in the arm every time I called him by his full name. My father is a straightforward, no nonsense sort of guy who's been working at Carl's Salvage Yard since graduating high school. My mother worked on and off before having my brother and me but decided to stay home with us. My father's wages kept us just above the poverty line. Coleman was definitely not the land of plenty, so we fit right in.

Though we grew up poor, my brother and I never lacked fashionable clothes. Unfortunately, they were usually hand-me-downs from our older cousins, leaving us with clothes about five or six years past their prime. I will never forget my first pair of moon boots. They were completely gray except for the red and blue stripes on the side. The worst part was that they first belonged to my cousin Ginny, and she wasn't known for great hygiene. Looking down the dark, odiferous opening of the boot, I wondered what kind of creepy fungus awaited my size seven. One whiff was enough to realize Ginny had once claimed these boots as her own. As if wearing hand-me-downs wasn't bad enough, the fact that a few of them came from a girl made it even worse.

It was sometime during junior high, when kids are the most sensitive to their appearance, when I felt the pain of wearing dorky attire. The first cold morning in December that year left me no choice but to slip on the once fashionable moon boots. I realized I was in for a long day when the bus driver stared at my feet the entire time it took me to climb the three short steps onto the bus and walk two-thirds of the way down the aisle until I found a seat. Glancing over my shoulder, I caught a glimpse of her face in the enormous, oversized mirror above her head, head shaking side to side, furrowed brow and all, watching me search for a place to sit. Luckily, I was the first stop, so I kept my feet tucked under the seat all the way to school. Once I got off the bus, it was a different story. A few of the older kids took great pleasure in seeing my awkwardness in having to wear outdated moon boots. Like sharks smelling blood, they attacked me mercilessly for twenty minutes until the bell rang, signaling us to go inside. "Look, it's Neil Armstrong. Can I have your autograph? Where'd you park your space ship? My sister used to have a pair of boots like that…ten years ago!" Their laughter stung my soul for a lot longer than they realized.

As luck would have it, it was also the day I forgot to put my tennis shoes in my backpack, leaving me to wear these puffy gray, clod-hopping boots until I got home. It could have been worse. When Thad was younger, my mom had once made him wear a section of blue jean material over his snowsuit when he was in elementary school. Because he crawled around on his hands and knees all the time, playing with his cars and trucks, he was constantly wearing holes in the knees of his snowsuit. She had cut off the bottom portion of my dad's old blue jeans and fastened them to the outside of his snowsuit with rubber bands. While he knew better than to take them off around home, it was a matter of minutes before they were off after getting on the bus in the morning. "Are you wearing your leggings at school?" she'd ask him. He tried his best to lie, but he just couldn't fool Noreen Carter as she stood there holding his snow suit with fresh holes in the knees.

I learned from Thad's mistakes. When I pushed my cars and trucks around, I stayed off my knees. It may have looked kind of silly with my bottom in the air, keeping my knees off the ground, but at least I didn't have to fasten a section of old blue jeans to my snow pants.

Clearly, my mother enjoyed making her sons look like buffoons because she also, at one time, made us put old bread bags over the liner of our boots to keep our feet dry. What kind of child would delight in having plastic bags stick up out of the top his boots? Not this one. She never put bread bags in *her* boots! Maybe this was all part of her plan to toughen us up toward the cruel world waiting to greet us when we got older.

CHAPTER 3

First Day Jitters

Up to this point, I had always used Labor Day for its intended purpose: a day to rest and relax. My family usually stayed close to home. Occasionally, friends and family would stop by for no other reason than they too had nothing else to do. It was the only time my dad ever cooked anything. He took advantage of having an audience in an effort to display his domestic skills. Though he refused to ask for any assistance, he usually needed help getting the grill started, which on more than one occasion culminated in a huge ball of flames. He would turn on the burners and then fumble with the igniter, which had never worked properly. (When an entire year passes between grilling opportunities, it's easy to understand why he always had trouble.) Then, without fail, he'd go look for a lighter or matches, and all the while, the grill turned into a giant propane tank as the burners spewed forth the extremely flammable fuel. Throwing a match under the hood of the grill was always a joyous experience...for the rest of us. It was like a mini-version of the Hindenburg every September in our backyard. His singed eyebrows and burnt arm hairs served as a visible reminder to the dangers of backyard grilling.

But this year, as my first day of teaching approached, rest and relaxation were nowhere to be found. There were two things consuming much of my thoughts. For starters, I wanted my classroom to be ready. There would be no rest until things were in order. Secondly, the weather was turning unseasonably warm. Temperatures tend to hover in the seventies during September, but for some cruel and unusual reason, highs were expected to reach the mid-nineties. Not a good situation for a guy with over-active sweat glands. For those living in drier regions, temperatures in the nineties aren't a big deal, but in Michigan, warmer temperatures go hand-in-hand with very high levels of humidity. The very thought of physical activity was enough to cause tiny rivers of sweat to slide down my back and sides. There are some who welcome the warm temperatures, but I'm not one of them. Perhaps I'd appreciate it more if my armpits were more cooperative. They always seem to *turn it on* at the most inconvenient times. For example, my first and only date with Marcia Hibbledorf back in high school went down as a total disaster due to my *condition*. Stopping at Glen's, I ran into the bathroom to use the hand dryer to dehydrate my armpits. Pit stains the size of dinner plates took on a life of their own and seemed to get bigger every time I lifted my arm to look. Fortunately, there was a jacket under the passenger seat of my car. An oversized red satin jacket, complete with grease and oil marks, with big white letters spelling out my father's place of employment: *Carl's Salvage Yard*. I'm sure I looked silly picking her up wearing khaki shorts and a coat. The only possible thing I could have done to make myself look any more ridiculous was to pull my white socks up to my kneecaps. She never went out with me again, causing years of awkwardness, as I never quite knew how to walk by her in school. Should I look down and away and appear as insecure as I felt? Or try to make eye-contact, knowing full well she wouldn't be looking toward me anyway, thereby making me feel even more unsure of myself?

Guys like me can't just rely on our looks. If you're thinking tall, dark, and handsome, instead think Howdy Doody meets Richie Cunningham.

The week before school is usually set aside for teachers to attend workshops or spend time getting their rooms ready for the upcoming year. The only other obligation we had was to attend a faculty meeting where Don Boggins, our principal, was set to give his annual "Fire-up" speech a few days before the long Labor Day weekend. It was his attempt at getting us ready to soar into a new school year. I'd heard some of the teachers complaining about his long-windedness. Never while he was in close proximity, though. This was something I would notice more and more as time went by.

Walking into the library for the meeting, I noticed one chair remaining. Right in front, too. Looking at the clock, I realized I was a few minutes late. Not a great way to start off the new year. Sitting down, I looked at the faces of some of the people I would be getting to know over the next year. To my immediate right sat Julie Denkins, a kindergarten teacher. She was a little over four feet tall and almost as wide. Her thinning gray hair was evidence that retirement was within reach, but as I would hear her say time after time, "Until my Matthew gets through pre-med, I'll be teaching." In other words, she didn't want to be here; she had to be here. Even though the temperature outside was quite warm, Julie sat in a chair wearing her "kindergarten" clothes. It's funny how kindergarten teachers just sort of stand out from everyone else. Her light blue hi-top Reeboks with the Velcro strap at the top were the first indication. The other qualifier was her button-down sweater with the words *Kids...Just Love 'Em* written in childlike scrawling across the front. It was red with an embroidered blackboard taking up the majority of the front. The words of wisdom were written in what was made to look like chalk.

Fran Helman, my first grade teacher, was next to her. She was also reaching an age where her daily attire consisted primarily of stretch pants and colorful sweaters. She and Julie were friends. They had to be. They'd taught in adjacent rooms for almost twenty-five years.

Helen McGinnis, another elderly teacher, was off by herself. One of the crankiest, crabbiest teachers I ever had. With a face resembling a cross between a walrus and a warthog, her demeanor spoke volumes: LEAVE ME ALONE!

Another teacher, Gus Harble, was sitting at the very end of the row. He was the only other male teacher on staff. He, too, had been around a while. He sat slouching in his chair with arms folded. His face had "hurry-up-and-get-this-over-with" written all over it. When I was in school, the kids always secretly called him Mr. Hairball. Occasionally somebody would slip and call him that to his face. Talk about fireworks. He'd get so mad. Personally, I thought it was kind of entertaining.

Sitting in front of Gus was Kim Busche. She was also from Coleman and had graduated two years ahead of me. She was the homecoming queen, class president, and whatever else her little heart desired. She was fairly good-looking too. But unfortunately, she knew it, which made finding her attractive, or even liking her, very difficult. Any girl who *thinks* she's good-looking automatically becomes a bit less so. I didn't care at all for her in high school, and it seemed her aura of snootiness had only intensified with the passing of time. She went out with a lot of guys, but it usually only took one or two dates before her suitors realized her favorite subject was herself. She's one of those people who has to have everything perfect, and if it's not, everyone will know it. One of those people who gets bent out of shape if even the slightest detail isn't quite right. One of those people who makes me want to gag.

"I'd like to introduce Ted Carter," Boggins said as it appeared everyone who was supposed to be there, was. "How many of you had Ted as a student?" he asked right off the bat. I saw a few arms elevate, and I quickly made eye-contact with those teachers before swiftly averting my gaze towards the floor. For whatever reason, it was a little awkward, especially between Fran Helman and myself. I had dated her daughter for a few weeks in high school and had dumped her for no other reason than she said the word *like* all the time. After a while, I didn't even listen to what she was saying except to count the number of times she said *that* word. Fran gave me a short smile before I looked down at the floor. Boggins continued, "We're glad you're here, Ted. Welcome back to Coleman."

"As you're all aware," Boggins went on to say, "we are at the beginning of another school year. This will be my thirty-second year at the helm," he rambled. As soon as he said that, I tried to figure out how old he was. My guess, around sixty. Funny thing was, he didn't look all that different fifteen years ago. Eyebrows like fat, furry caterpillars draped over his beady eyes. Dark brown hair haloed around the perimeter of his head. The top of his head held a very shiny glaze, like he'd taken car wax and buffed his head every morning. Looking at the top of his head, I tried to imagine how slippery it must be, wondering how difficult it would be to keep a hat from sliding down over his eyes with that smooth finish. Did his wife help with the buffing? My mind wandered into an imaginary commercial for car wax with Boggins' head as one of the props.

I could see he was talking, but my mind was racing a million miles an hour. There was so much to do in my room. In between imaginary situations, I started to write down things that needed doing in my classroom when all of a sudden I heard, "Right, Ted?" Deer-in-the-headlights would be the most fitting phrase to explain how I felt at that moment.

Slightly befuddled, I said, "Um, right," not totally grasping what it was I was either agreeing with or volunteering to do. Feeling the stares of my colleagues, my face flushed warm. I wasn't sure if Boggins was really asking me a question or if he was trying to embarrass me a little due to my lack of active listening. He rambled on for another half hour before giving us a five-minute break. Upon returning to the library, I noticed a few empty chairs. Boggins' spiel wasn't exactly blowing my mind, so I understood why some of them passed on the opportunity to come back. During our break, I noticed Gus Harble walking down the hallway, either going back to his room or perhaps taking a trip the lavatory. Fran and Julie were still in the hallway talking about their summer vacations. Julie was describing a cottage she had rented this past summer with her husband, and she kept going on and on about the specifics of the occasion. Both of these women were *detail* people. It seemed their stories took longer to tell than the actual event they were describing.

Though Boggins carried on for another half hour, I had no idea what point he was trying to make. Gus Harble did in fact return, but only with five minutes left. I gave him the benefit of the doubt. Probably spending some quality time in the bathroom. (He did have the latest copy of *Sports Illustrated* is his hand.)

Finally, Boggins wrapped it up. "Have a great year, everyone," he said. "Get some rest; you know how tough that first day back can be." Before he even finished his sentence, the scraping of chairs, the rustling of papers, the cracking of old joints, and the sound of people talking made it clear this meeting was adjourned.

When I finally got back to my room, I looked at all that had to be done. Even though a considerable amount of my time had been spent at school over the last week, it didn't look like much had been accomplished. An avalanche of ideas and to-dos had cascaded through my brain, leaving me totally overwhelmed. My checklist had very few check marks. As soon as I started one thing, my mind raced to something else that *had* to be done. In the middle of that task, my brain would think of something else, explaining why there were so many unfinished projects lying around my room. After several more hours, I finally felt content enough to leave.

Before walking out to the parking lot, I wandered down the hall to the huge glass double doors my students would use to enter the school. The same double doors I had used as a kid. Pushing open the doors with the bright afternoon sun blasting in my eyes, I laughed to myself. Looking off to the left, I spotted the exact location where I used to wait in line. My smile broadened just a bit as I stood there and remembered the time I unknowingly squished part of my own lunch as I waited with my classmates for our teacher to signal us to come inside. Standing there in line as a young adolescent, I'd happened to look down and see a sandwich neatly placed inside a small, clear plastic bag. For some unknown reason, I used my foot to squash it into a fine mush. *Some poor sap is going to be very hungry by the end of the day,* I thought to myself. Had I known the poor sap was me, I would have made a better decision. I realized it was my sandwich when I opened my lunch box and saw only an apple and a juice box.

The only other person still in the building was Frank Tisdale, the custodian. He looked like he was closing in on ninety. No one is sure how long he's been working here at Coleman, but my best guess would be somewhere close to fifty years. He worked here when my parents went to school, and I'm pretty sure I remember my grandma mentioning something about him once, so his tenure is one of our town's mysteries. "See you later, Frank," I said, walking past him in the hallway.

"Take care, Buddy," he said back. He called everyone Buddy. Even women. I had seen him quite a bit over the past several days while getting my room ready. He never seemed to accomplish anything that benefited the school, unless shoveling his mouth full of potato chips and playing solitaire at a little table in the boiler room is considered constructive.

Some time ago, I asked, "Hey, Frank, would it be possible to attach the pencil sharpener to the wall in my room?" Three days later, it was sitting on my desk, still in the box.

Walking out of the building and noticing that my car and Frank's old Buick were the only ones left in the parking lot, left me feeling slightly dejected. *It'll be nice to get a few years under my belt; then maybe I won't have to put in all this time before school starts.* The first bell, signaling the start of school, had yet to ring, but I was already feeling frazzled.

There's nothing quite like the first day of school. What many people don't realize is that it's a coin toss as to who's more nervous, the children or the teachers. What if my class is totally out of control? What happens when I try to get their attention and they keep right on talking? What if I raise my arms during a passionate moment and my shirt is drenched with sweat from my elbows to waistline? What if they call me Mr. Farter? So many *what-ifs*.

The drive home provided some comfort. It was only ten or twelve minutes from parking lot to driveway, allowing enough time to unwind a bit and think nothing of the responsibilities lying ahead. Flipping the radio dial to WKIL, "Flying High Again" by Ozzy Osbourne was just what my mind needed to escape reality. I had blown the factory speakers a long time ago, allowing me the opportunity to install one giant speaker that took up the entire back seat. Hearing loss was a small price to pay for having the opportunity to feel like I was front and center at a stadium rock show. Looking up in the rear view mirror, watching it thump and jiggle in time with the bass, freed my mind of current worries. It was somewhat difficult to see clearly, but the right corner of my mouth slowly ascended into a half-smile. In an approving manner, I gave myself a wink and a nod as a way of assuring myself things were going to be just fine.

There was enough time before supper to read the newspaper and watch a little television, giving my mind a needed break.

After supper, I went down to the basement, which has remained unfinished for nearly thirty years. The cobwebs and stacks of boxes were a testament to that. I'd managed to clear a small area where I could comfortably play my guitar without fear of having anyone actually hear me. While I was in college, using money from a student loan, I'd purchased myself a fine instrument. The quality of my guitar and the quality of my voice were on opposite ends of the spectrum. With the help of a friend, we'd gone to Lansing and made the big purchase at an upper-echelon guitar dealer. It was a used Guild guitar. Made in the U.S.A. A little out of my league, but one I'd be happy to try and play up to.

There's something about the feel of an acoustic guitar. Whether strumming or simply plucking the strings, guitar playing has always provided one with the opportunity to forget about the rigors of life. That is, if you can make the chords correctly. I spent many dateless Friday and Saturday nights in college, practicing. (There are some benefits to having a lackluster social life.) I'd spent a long time working at learning to play properly. Many times when I started learning to play, the fingertips of my left hand would radiate in pain as I forced the strings down on the fretboard. An indented groove running across the tips of my fingers served as a badge of honor for all the hours spent practicing. For anyone not familiar with playing guitar, it's like taking your fingertips and pressing them down on a cheese slicer…for hours. The pain would eventually subside. The lines and indentations ended up being replaced by calluses. Calluses, with their tough, ornery thickness, made it much easier to press down the strings, therefore making it easier to play. When your fingertips have reached the callus-point, you've arrived, because the worst part is behind you. The next time you hear Bryan Adams sing, "played it 'til my fingers bled," from "Summer of '69," know he's not too far off.

I've never been one to want stardom, but it is nice to imagine playing in front of an audience of a few thousand. I know that would never happen. Too nervous. Opening my mouth to sing led to a sound more like a squeaky fan belt. Playing in the basement, where no one can listen, is fine for now. If I even pretend someone's listening, my palms get sweaty, and my voice gets all pitchy. Nope, best just to play it safe. I'll do the vocals in my head for now.

As evening approached, my parents settled into their assigned seats on the couch and recliner directly in front of the TV. Feeling somewhat anxious, I stretched out on the floor, like I'd done so many times before, and whittled away the hours before bed in a vegetative state.

During the night, with my mind racing through hypothetical situations, it was a constant battle to stay asleep. I woke up at 2:58 a.m., tossing and turning, at which point I immediately did a subtraction problem in my head. If I fall asleep right now, I'll get almost three more hours of sleep. There were similar problems that night (3:14 a.m., 4:32 a.m., 4:45 a.m., and 5:27 a.m.). Somewhere in there, a dream floated through my mind. It was more like a nightmare. I was in my classroom trying to teach. There were kids in the room, but I couldn't see their faces. I was trying to get them to settle down, but nobody seemed to be listening. I raised my voice to get their attention. Nothing. It was like they were totally ignoring me. Slightly annoyed, I raised my voice even more, just a notch or two below full-fledged yelling. "Everybody needs to sit down… right now." Instead of motivating them to find their seats and start paying attention, the room was quickly filled with shrieks of laughter. Kids were laughing and pointing…at me. I had absolutely no control. When I woke up and realized it was only a dream, there was some relief. Not much, though. I finally settled into a deep sleep, only to have the alarm go off at exactly 6:00 a.m. *Why couldn't I have been this tired six hours ago?*

Stumbling into the bathroom, I kicked my dad's underwear out of the way. What keeps him from picking it up himself and putting it in the dirty clothes basket is one of our family's greatest mysteries. It always sat in the same spot due to a rather unfortunate mishap several years ago. While shedding his skivvies, his big toe got caught in the waistband, causing him to stumble forward and whack his head against the bathroom sink. No one was overly concerned about him until later that night at supper, while sitting across the table from Thad, when he asked, "Who are you?" So now his shower ritual includes sitting down along the edge of the bathtub to remove his underwear.

Not wanting to waste valuable time, my clothes were already lying out, and my lunch had been packed with leftovers the night before, leaving me a few extra minutes to bask in the splendor of a hot shower. Realizing a way to make the shower last even longer, I pulled the curtain aside, reached across the floor to the small bathroom drawer below the one my parents used, and grabbed my shaving supplies, leaving small puddles of water on the floor. The tiled wall near the shower head held a shaving mirror, fastened by three small suction cups. Once I wiped away the condensation, I could see my face in greater detail. Turning to the left, I preceded to fill my dominant hand with shaving cream and lather up with the creamy white foam. The razor slid over my cheek like a puck on ice. After going over my face once, I moved in to get a better glimpse of my work. It wasn't uncommon for me to miss a few places, especially the area between my nose and upper lip. Turning the razor upside down to go over this area again, I felt a sudden sting of pain. The razor had stuck firmly in my flesh. Three thin lines of blood came rising to the surface. *Just great! This was the last thing I needed to have happen.* After getting out of the shower, I applied a small section of toilet paper. Little red dots quickly appeared. Unrolling a larger portion, I hurriedly folded it and applied it to the still burning section of my face.

"What happened to you?" my mother asked as I walked out of the bathroom toward my room. Without saying a word, I tilted my head to the side and gave her a *Why-do-you-insist-on-asking-me-questions-you-already-know-the-answer-to* glare. Shuffling past her, I shut my bedroom door a little harder than intended. Getting dressed proved tricky in an effort to avoid getting blood spots on my clean shirt.

Throughout breakfast, I kept changing the toilet paper. Finally, after several minutes, a scab began to form. I had been in this situation before. Past experience told me, *Whatever you do, DON'T PICK AT IT!*

With thin lines of crusty blood, I was tempted to lodge the razor into the other half of my upper lip to even things out. It didn't look too bad if I turned slightly to the right. *Great! Just what I need. Now I can spend the whole day trying to keep my class from seeing my entire left half. That shouldn't be too hard.*

My mother makes coffee every morning, and for much of my life I've refrained from getting into the coffee habit. However, because I didn't want to fall asleep during my first day as a teacher, I grabbed a ceramic coffee cup from the cupboard, poured in some high-octane coffee, and added enough cream and sugar to make it taste more like a coffee milkshake. I've always loved the smell of fresh coffee, but having coffee breath and brown teeth is what kept me from making it a morning custom.

By the time I finished and walked out to my car, it was ten after seven. A little behind schedule, but not too bad. Once I got out on the road and had the radio tuned, I rolled down the window to get a little breeze across my face. *This is really it,* I thought to myself. *This is for real.* A few minutes into my drive I started to rehearse how I would introduce myself to my students. Once that was determined, I looked up in the rearview mirror and gave myself another affirming nod.

What happened next can best be described as a catastrophe. About halfway to school, I noticed a small lump up ahead in the road. Before my eyes could make out exactly what it was, my nose caught one whiff...skunk. Everyone knows the smart thing to do is go around it. Veering left, my rear tire went right over a huge pothole, immediately blowing the tire to smithereens. *Just great! Could this day get any worse?* Pulling off the road, I just sat there in shock for a moment, wishing a pit crew would jump out of the ditch and change my tire. The clock on my radio read 7:38 a.m., reminding me that I was a bit behind schedule, and therefore forcing me to actually get out of the car to change the tire. Loosening my tie and rolling up the sleeves of my shirt, I made my way to the trunk. Sliding a half a quart of oil, two bungee cords, and a jug of windshield washer solvent out of the way, I managed to get the car jack and tire iron out. Trying to get the lug nuts off proved to be a little more difficult than originally anticipated. Apparently, the last time I put the lug nuts on, I had cross-threaded them, making them nearly impossible to remove. It was the equivalent of trying to pull a pacifier from an alligator. I vaguely remember thinking to myself at the time, *I'll let the next guy worry about it.* By the time I got all the lug nuts off, my shirt had more dark areas than light. I could feel a wet spot on my back about the size of a placemat. I knew better than to look under my pits. *Just fantastic*, I thought. *Now I have sweat stains the size of Montana to go along with my Hitler moustache.* By the time the spare tire was put on, it was 7:52. I wasn't quite ready for NASCAR, but despite all that had happened, I was somewhat surprised at how quickly I'd gotten the job done. Had the air-conditioning in my car worked properly, I might have dried out before arriving at school.

Pulling into the parking lot *after* the busses had already unloaded was not part of the plan. I ran to my classroom and immediately sat down. Taking my shirt off and draping it over my chair, I glanced around the room, looking at twenty-seven empty desks that were going to be filled with twenty-seven inquiring minds in less than five minutes. *What in the world am I going to do?* Sometimes feelings of self-doubt have a way of creeping up on you when you're least able to deal with them.

My pulse was just about back to normal when I heard it. *BRRRRRRRIIIIIIINNNNGGG!!!!!!* It was 8:05 and time to begin. Quickly putting my shirt back on, I headed out of my room, down the hallway towards my students.

"Are you hot?"

That was the first question some kid asked me when I went out the double doors to meet my class. I decided not to answer, not because I didn't want to; I just couldn't quite come up with anything clever. A simple *yes* or *no* didn't seem to be enough. The thought of grabbing this kid by the neck and sticking his face in my armpit had crossed my mind.

"What happened to your face?" asked a boy who was almost as tall as I was.

"Just a little shaving accident," I replied.

"Does it hurt?" he continued.

"No, not really."

"My dad hacks his face up all the time."

"Is that right?" I said, turning around to walk back to my classroom.

"Yeah, but he doesn't live with us anymore."

"Oh, that's too bad." Boy, this kid was talkative. I don't remember being that chatty with my teachers on the first day.

"Well, it's okay. He was hitting my mom a lot, so he had to go live somewhere else."

"Uh...this isn't really the best time to be talking about this kind of stuff," I told him in an effort to get him to stop talking. The thought of ignoring him crossed my mind, but I didn't want to be rude.

Making our way into the room, I couldn't believe the moment for which I had worked so hard was finally here. Despite my nerves, I did my best to stay calm and not give them the impression that I was within striking distance of wetting myself.

"Good morning, boys and girls," I announced as they all filed in to find their seats.

"I hope you had a great summer. I'm really looking forward to getting to know each and every one of you this year." I went on for a while with the usual *welcome* stuff that I remember previous teachers doing. I really can't remember everything I said, except that at times I was more worried about keeping my left half turned away from the class all the while keeping my arms at my sides just in case the pit stains weren't totally dry. I was in the middle of learning one of my first lessons as a teacher: It's kind of hard to stand up in front of a bunch of kids and talk while focusing on something else.

"Are we going to do anything fun this year?" came a voice belonging to a little red haired girl with freckles.

"Well," I said, "that depends on you. If you're the kind of person who likes to have fun, then you'll probably have a great year."

"So what you're saying is that if I want to have fun, then I can just go ahead and do it?" she asked.

"Well, no...not exactly," I stammered. "What I meant was that how much fun you have and how much you enjoy school depends a lot on you." *What in the world am I talking about?* Her face went from a look of wonder to a look of confusion. "What I mean is that if you want to have fun, you'll have to create those opportunities for yourself." *Why couldn't I have just said, "Yes, hopefully we'll have a lot of fun this year?"*

Gathering my thoughts, I said, "The first thing I need to do is take attendance. When I say your name, please raise your hand."

After reading through the names, it dawned on me that even though I had a sheet of paper with their names on it, that wasn't going to help me know who was who throughout the day. Walking over to grab a sheet of notebook paper off my desk, I began to make a seating chart. The room was dead silent for about twelve seconds when all of a sudden they all started talking to each other. At first it wasn't too bad, but it quickly escalated into a full-blown racket. Kids were screaming to each other from one side of the room to the other. I really didn't want to start the year by yelling at them to quiet down. Perhaps if I just started talking, maybe they would quiet down on their own.

I continued with my "Welcome Back" speech. "Anyway, I'd like to welcome you all to sixth grade." I paused for a second to see if would take effect. Nothing. It was as if I wasn't even in the room. "Boys and girls," I said a little louder, "I'd like to welcome you back to school. My name is Mr. Carter, and I'll be your teacher this year." Still nothing. It was quickly turning into an awkward situation. I could see that I was going to have to raise my voice to get their attention. "Ladies and gentlemen," I demanded, "stop talking." Waiting for a second I said a little louder, "I need your attention up here, right now! That is the third time I've started talking. You need to be quiet so I can continue with what it is I need to say."

There were some glances around the room. Some of the kids looked scared, but it was clear there were others who seemed to enjoy getting a rise out of me. I had planned to tell them a little about myself, how I also had attended this school, how I had actually been in this room as a student, but due to my agitated state, I forgot.

I'd always heard the phrase: *Don't smile until Christmas*, and that's exactly what I planned to do. Of course, I wanted the kids to like me, but that would come later. My education classes taught me that the first few weeks of school are all about getting routines and expectations established. My vision of what these children could become sent shivers down my spine. I began to picture all twenty-seven students listening attentively, hanging on my every word. I'd ask questions, they'd have answers. I got goose bumps imagining the dialogue we could have.

"Boys and girls, as we think about the impact of European colonization on Native Americans, what would you consider to be the most damaging?" I'd ask.

"Well, Mr. Carter, that's a difficult question to answer. I mean, if you look at the short-term effects, you could say that sickness and disease were definitely a major issue. However, when you look at the problem long-term, the broken treaties and deceitfulness of the white man have had an extremely devastating result not only on their customs, but on their entire way of life that has lasted for generations," some beaming, bright-eyed young child would respond.

This is so grand. So wonderful. I can't believe I get paid to do this!

My hopeful vision lasted for no more than one half hour. While I was going over some of the daily procedures and what I expected from my class, I noticed a few students at the back of the room engaged in some kind of commotion. I couldn't see exactly what they were doing, but it looked like one of the boys, Bryan Brookens, had started using his pencil as a pool stick. He apparently decided to engage some of his neighbors in a friendly game of billiards. This is not how today was supposed to go down. I didn't really want to start screaming and yelling this early, but apparently that's what this situation required. "Excuse me, gentlemen," I said a little louder than I had previously been speaking. "Can I have your eyes and ears up here, please? I'm going over some important stuff right now that's in your best interest to listen to."

Then, in an extremely loud and irritating tone, Bryan said, "What?" His face curled into a distorted, scrunched up kind of expression. "What I'd do? I'm not doing anything!"

"It looks like you're playing some sort of game back there," I said.

"I'm listening," he sassed. "How about gettin' off my back?"

"Excuse me," I demanded. "I'm talking up here, and when I'm talking, you need to be listening."

"Whatever."

"Excuse me. You can leave right now!" I shouted. I was ticked. Looking around, some of the rest of the class really seemed to be enjoying themselves. They weren't exactly rolling on the floor, but the smirks on their faces told me this was some kind of game, and they were serious about winning. My face was burning with anger, and they seemed to enjoy having front row seats to all the action.

Bryan slowly got up and scuffled toward the door. The room was dead quiet.

I felt like I was in a dream. A bad dream. *This wasn't how things were supposed to go down!*

As I showed him where to sit in the hallway, I felt the urge to let him know that I was not the kind of teacher he wanted to mess with. "When you come into this room, you will show me some respect, got it? I am not going deal with this kind of garbage all year, do you understand me? Now you can sit out here for the next fifteen minutes and start thinking about how you're going to act in this classroom." *Man, I was good. There ain't no way I'm going to have some poor excuse for a human being show me up in my own classroom and make my life miserable.*

"All right," I said, stepping back into the classroom. "I will not tolerate that kind of behavior in my classroom. If any of you think you can come in here and disrupt the learning process, you are sadly mistaken. As a matter of fact, if you're not going to give me your best, then you might as well stay home." I had recently watched *Hoosiers* again, and Gene Hackman's character was the kind of teacher I emulated. *If you don't like how I do things, get out.* "It doesn't do this class any good to have people in here being a distraction and getting in the way of someone's education," I went on. "You are here to learn, I'm here to teach, and that's exactly what I intend to do." As I was talking, I made my way to the back of the room. "I'm watching you," I said under my breath to the scrubs who had been fooling around earlier. "You guys better get your act together, or you're not going to be in here." I was so close to one boy's face, I could smell his crusty morning breath. The funny thing is that when I said, *"You're not going to be in here,"* their faces lit up like Christmas trees.

I consider myself to be a pretty reasonable person. I'll fight for what's important, and right now having their attention was pretty dog-gone important.

Not much of what I'd planned on that first day went *as planned.* I found myself doing a lot more talking than I really wanted. The more I talked, the less interested they seemed to be. By mid-afternoon, it was hard to say who was more bored, them or me. I knew it was going to be tough, but I had to get these kids to understand the importance of doing what was expected of them. "When you walk in the room, I need you to sit down right away. I'll have something on your desk for you to work on, and I expect that you'll get working on it right away. This is not the time for fooling around; that's supposed to happen at recess." Gaining momentum, I rambled on for several minutes. During my afternoon spiel, three kids fell asleep, giving me the opportunity to kick the leg of their desk as I strolled up and down the rows.

Somewhere in the middle of the afternoon, the sun positioned itself at just the right angle, causing it to send out beams of intense heat and light into the room. The rays were magnified by the glass window. It was like being trapped in a dryer with a bunch of wet towels. The thought of wearing only a loincloth danced through my head. *That would get 'em to pay attention.*

I just about blew a gasket towards the end of the day as I handed out a half sheet of paper for my students to put their name and phone numbers on before leaving for the day. "Put your name at the top. I need you to print it too. Skip a line and then put your home phone number below your name, please."

As their heads bowed and their pencils began writing, a hand belonging to the largest boy in my class, Steven Dooley, slowly ascended. "What are we supposed to do with this half sheet of paper?" he asked.

Are you serious? What on earth have you been doing back there? Besides listening, that is. Due to my uptight condition, I was physically unable to speak. The only thing left to do was glare. Had my eyes been able to shoot death rays, this boy would be nothing but a smoldering lump of flesh on the floor by his desk.

After what seemed like an eternity, the clock finally made its way to 3:30 p.m. My first day was over. I wasn't sure how I felt, except tired. While my vision of what was supposed to happen had a slight derailment, I was still optimistic about tomorrow. I knew these kids needed a "firm" hand as I guided them toward my idea of what I thought they should become. *Psychology 101.* Punish, reward. Punish, reward until I had them eating out of my hand. During student teaching, my cooperating teacher had his class following orders so well, I wasn't sure if I was in a school or West Point Academy. The "firm" manner in which he taught worked for him, and I had no reason to think it wouldn't work for me.

CHAPTER 4

Who Are These People?

After spending a considerable amount of time at the end of the day getting ready for day two, I stopped by Gretchen's for something cold.

"How's that first day, Teach?" she asked as I sat down on a worn barstool.

"Not bad," I moaned. "A little tired, but you know how it is. You gotta train 'em on those first few days," I said in a tone masking the uncertainty inside.

"Train 'em how?" she asked.

"Well, you know, you gotta train them when to raise their hands, how to leave for lunch, when to use the bathroom, who the boss is... stuff like that."

"Is that right?"

"Yeah, according to what I learned in college, you have to be tough on those first few days. It's a lot easier to soften up later on in the year than it is to try and get tough. Don't worry, Gretchen, I'll show 'em my soft side one of these days."

I finished my drink and headed home thinking about my first day. I couldn't believe I was *actually* a teacher. I wondered if I was going to feel this tired and sore at the end of every day. My feet were killing me. The backs of my legs felt like they had been squeezed by a pair of giant vice grips. Each step reminded me that summer was over.

Pulling into the driveway of my parents' house, I felt a sense of relief. I knew what was waiting for me inside. As tradition would have it, a plate of cookies, hopefully still warm, and a glass of ice cold milk would be setting on the counter; I just knew it. My mother always used to make cookies for my brother and me on our first day of school. Usually chocolate chip.

Grasping the door knob, I quickly realized the door was locked. *Oh shoot!* My dad had replaced the door a year ago, and I never thought to have a key made for myself. Until now, of course. Realizing there was nothing I could do, I found a shady spot under the large maple tree by the side of the house to sit under. Before closing my eyes, I focused momentarily on the crumpled siding below our living room window and laughed.

When Thad was about ten, he thought it would be cool to put a baseball card in the rear tire of his bike, in hopes of making it sound more like a motorcycle. Up and down the driveway he went. In all the excitement, as he propelled forward, his curiosity got the better of him and trumped his ability to make logical decisions. For a few seconds he turned back to watch the card *rat-a-tat-tat* in the spokes. The wrinkled siding has since served as a visual reminder of his not-so-graceful stop.

I'd forgotten that Tuesdays are the days my mother goes grocery shopping. That's when Glen's has double-coupon day. I wasn't sure how long I'd been asleep, but it was seemingly enough time for my arm to go to sleep as well.

"Whatchyadoin', honey?" my mother asked as she got out of the car, which woke me up. "That's kind of a weird place to take a nap, isn't it?"

Because my brain was fried, I said nothing as we walked toward the side door.

"How was that first day?" she asked once we got inside.

"Oh, pretty good," I managed to say.

"How many kids do you have?"

"Twenty-seven," I replied.

"Wow, that's a big class for Coleman."

She was right. It was a big class for Coleman. Twelve years ago, a pretty hard winter made its stay for about three and a half months. With temperatures way below normal and several feet of snow on the ground, sometimes days would go by before people could get out of their driveways. Because Coleman lies in a valley, most folks get terrible reception on their TV's unless they have one of those huge antennas bolted to the roof of their house. Apparently, cold weather and poor signals are a perfect combination for snuggling. The result of all that love now filled my classroom.

Grabbing the newspaper from the front porch, I dawdled away the time before dinner by pretending to read it.

"Come and get it," my mother yelled from the kitchen. She had to say it loud enough so my dad could hear her from the garage. For the second time in less than a week, she served meatloaf, baked potato, and cooked carrots. The once bright orange carrots were now a light brownish gray. The baked potatoes had been cooked in the microwave, meaning they were probably still hard in the middle. The meatloaf sat there frowning in the 9 x 13 glass dish, hoping someone or something would just put it out of its misery. A canned jar of pineapple rings sat patiently on the counter next to the stove. Dessert.

As usual, there was very little conversation around the table, with the exception of someone asking for a bowl or dish that happened to be just out of reach.

"Well, son, since you're working full time and living with us, your mother and I decided it's only fair to charge you a little rent for living here," my father said to me between bites of his baked potato at supper. Using the same hand which held his fork, he wiped a glob of sour cream from his upper lip and continued, "I know how much you teachers make, and there's no sense in giving you a free ride, Mr. Big Shot."

I could have told him that he currently made more than I do, but it would have fallen on deaf ears.

"Well, that's fine," I said. "I planned on giving you something until I found a place of my own." Believe me, the thought of sitting down every night with these two people was all the motivation I needed.

I grabbed a piece of bread and began spreading butter around.

"For Pete's sake, how much butter do you need for one slice of bread?" my mother insisted. "There's enough on there for three slices."

Ignoring her, my teeth sank into the heavily coated slice of bread. Upon pulling it away from my mouth, there were huge teeth marks left behind.

"Would you like me to scrape some back in the margarine container?" I asked sarcastically as a soggy chunk of buttered bread flew out of my mouth.

"For crying out loud, Noreen, leave the boy alone. We'll just charge more rent to help cover the cost of his eating habits," my father laughed, showing partially chewed chunks of potato. The sour cream really made his teeth look bad. Years of steady coffee consumption and chewing tobacco had done some pretty heavy damage. He didn't care. Who did he have to impress?

My parents had been married thirty-six years. Each year brought a steady decline towards complacency. My father worked in an auto salvage yard. The highlight of his day was seeing a wrecked Chevy come in on the back of a flatbed. His proudest moment in life was graduating from high school. Besides marrying my mother, his only other major accomplishment was taking second place in the Hay-Bale-Toss competition during Town & Country Days a few years ago. His bald head was covered by thin wisps of hair starting just above his left ear and combed completely across the top of his head to just above his right ear. Every time the wind blew more than ten miles per hour, he walked with his hand on top of his head to keep the hairs in place. The hair sprouting out of his ears had more density than what was growing on top of his noggin.

"You know, that's not a bad idea, Marv," she said, looking at me. "We certainly could use a little help with the grocery bill."

It didn't matter how much she had to spend on food, it was never enough. You would have thought my mother lived through the Great Depression the way she rationed food. She took the serving suggestion on the side of the containers literally. If one serving of potato chips was considered twelve chips, that's what you were served. Anything more than that was being gluttonous. Years ago my brother and I realized that if we sent our mom to the fridge for something, we could usually help ourselves to more rations when she bent down to retrieve the desired item. Once in a while, we'd hit pay dirt. She'd have to go downstairs for something, and that was when we'd pert near choke to death shoving handfuls of french fries or extra spoonfuls of applesauce into our mouths. After she caught on to our little game, she made us get things ourselves.

During high school, our house got TP'd with toilet paper. Most people just let it biodegrade on the tree limbs, but not us. My mom was out there the next morning with a broom handle, collecting the toilet paper into one gigantic roll. Using a step ladder, she got most of it out of the tree limbs. I remember hoping so hard that no one would drive by while she was out there. She salvaged enough for several weeks, but because it had gotten damp, its durability and softness were greatly compromised, causing us to wrap our hand like King Tut in order for it be effective.

Sadly, mealtime at our house was less than a joyous occasion. Most of the time, we'd sit around in dead silence except for the noises our mouths made as we chewed our food or someone asked someone to pass the tater tots. Sometimes the silence was broken by my father's burps between bites. *BUMP-UH* . The BU- part sounded like someone gave him a little sucker punch to the stomach. When he got to the −MP part, his lips flapped and vibrated together for a micro-second. The −UH was stretched out a little longer and closely resembled the sound a Tupperware container makes when you lift the edge of the lid while pressing down in the middle. If my mother happened to be in a good mood, she would quite often say, "Bring it up again, Marv, and we'll vote on it." I never really understood what that meant, but I always found it hard to suppress a chuckle.

My parents weren't genuinely interested in the finer details that happened in either my life or my brother's. They'd ask how our day went. We'd say "good" and that was all they really wanted to hear. *How was school?* "Good." *Did you learn anything interesting today?* "No, not really." Once when I was in middle school, my father asked how my day went, so I started to tell him about a science experiment my class had done. About halfway through my recap, he remembered that he needed to call Carl, his boss, and ask to leave a few minutes early because he had a doctor's appointment, leaving me to wonder why he had asked in the first place.

So there we sat, the three of us. My brother had escaped almost two years ago. Marriage was his ticket out. He couldn't take it anymore. He was tired of sneaking behind the house between meals to scarf down a bag of Doritos or empty the entire contents of a box of Little Debbie snack cakes down his throat. He wanted his freedom. He wanted to be able to sit down at the table and take as much as he wanted of something without having to hear what a pig he was making of himself.

"Don't forget, Marv, you've got a meeting tonight at seven," my mom said, breaking the silence.

"Is it the first Tuesday already?" Dad mumbled.

"You've got about ten minutes to get there," she added. If that was supposed to motivate him, it didn't work.

My father belonged to one of the oldest organizations in Coleman, the Sons of Encouragement, which met on the first Tuesday night each month at the Coleman Civic Center. It was started in 1917 by a group of men, young and old alike, unable to serve in World War I for a variety of reasons. Motivated by equal parts shame and guilt, they took it upon themselves to do something significant while their counterparts dodged bullets and grenades half a world away. In the beginning, they raised funds to help support the troops with everyday items such as coffee, soap, toothpaste, and socks. With the passing of each generation, the Sons of Encouragement slowly descended away from its original purpose and developed into social hour for a group of older men with negative views of government and politics. Their sole purpose was to eat, drink coffee, and complain about elected officials at the state and national levels. The fluctuating price of a gallon of regular unleaded was another hot topic.

Their annual fundraiser, which took place during Town & Country Days in July, was a pork barbecue dinner. The dinner consisted of a moderate portion of barbecued pork, a dinner roll, approximately two tablespoons of coleslaw that hardly anyone ate, and a small Styrofoam cup filled about two-thirds of the way up with watered-down lemonade. They barely raised enough money to cover the cost of renting the basement at the Civic Center for their Tuesday night meetings, putting an end to their philanthropic ways long ago.

These suppertime rituals often made me wonder if I was adopted. Were these two people really my parents? To say my family is strange would be putting it mildly. This was verified when I was a kid and had gone over to Clip's house one afternoon. We'd been passing some pretty heavy gas (school pizza... need I say more?). His mother walked into his bedroom where we were playing Legos and said, "All right, boys, if you're going to keep ripping farts in here, either go outside or shut the door." I could not believe his mother said that word. We never would have said that at our house. I'm not sure whose idea it was, probably my mother's, but we were forced to use terms like *toot* and *stinker*. Once, when our family was traveling downstate in our station wagon, my brother asked if I had *beefed*. If looks could kill, he would have been dead because my mother gave him her *death glare,* complete with pursed lips, furrowed brow, and flared nostrils.

It was just past seven o'clock. With my dad gone for a few hours, my mom was left to watch *Wheel of Fortune* and *Jeopardy* alone. With only one television in our house, it was either watch what they watched or find something else to do. In my exhausted state, I gathered what little strength I had and quietly made my way to bed.

Chapter 5

Losing Control

Going to bed at 7:30 p.m. was a huge mistake, but I couldn't help it. I was exhausted. Later that night, after getting almost eight hours of sleep, I was wide awake, and it was only three-thirty in the morning. I tossed and turned until 4:30 a.m. Then, I decided to get up and get something done. Being careful not to disturb my parents, I tip-toed through the house, though my father was usually up around this time—staggering into the bathroom to take care of some business.

Stepping out of the shower, I proceeded to dry off. Since my shaving wound from yesterday was still fresh, I bypassed the opportunity to shave. Using my silver hairbrush, I began putting my hair in place. The same place it's been since seventh grade: parted on the left. The little transistor radio we kept on the bathroom counter was quietly emitting a little background music. I quickly changed the station to WKIL, as this was the only time I got to listen to it in the bathroom. My mom likes the light stuff, so I took advantage of the opportunity to listen to something that wasn't going to induce me into a comatose state. It was more than a little embarrassing that my dad walked in on me in the bathroom while I stood at the sink in my underwear, using a hairbrush to sing along to "Sweet Home Alabama." Shaking his head, he calmly shut the door and went back to his bedroom. This wasn't the first time he'd walked in on me doing something stupid. There were times, too numerous to mention, where he had caught me in compromising positions.

There wasn't any sense in waiting around the house for another hour, so I left for school. Getting there with two hours to spare was a complete turnaround from yesterday. Sitting down at my desk, I looked around the room. Looking at the desks arranged in neat little rows, I couldn't help but wonder who these kids really were. Sure, I'd gone to school with some of their family members, but I really knew very little about them. I could tell who came from good families and who didn't, but that was about it. Twenty-seven kids who were at that stage in life where they didn't like being treated like little children but who also weren't ready to handle many of the responsibilities that were given to older students. Somewhere in between. That was something I had in common with them. I was somewhere in between too. I felt like I was on an imaginary fulcrum with college on one side and acting like a real grown-up on the other. Most of my high school friends had moved on with their lives, except Clip, who still worked at Larry's Lumber helping customers load two-by-fours and plywood. Living with my parents certainly wasn't where I wanted to be, even though I did appreciate a *roof over my head*. Since I'd recently broken up with my college sweetheart, my social life consisted of watching television with my parents or going to Gretchen's by myself. Definitely not the Gentlemen's Quarterly representative I was hoping to project.

Sitting at my desk, my eyelids felt like little lead weights had been tied to them. Getting up so early and, of course, bypassing the coffee had me feeling a little droopy. The next thing I knew, the bell was ringing. It was 8:05 a.m.—time to get my students. Groggily, I walked out of my room into the hallway.

As the class piled into the room, I wanted to start out by saying something important, something grandiose. I wanted to capture their attention, say something that would blow their minds. When nothing came to me, I told them to open their math books to the first lesson.

There had been some snickering right off the bat. After several minutes, I couldn't stand it any longer. "What's so funny?" I asked in a very matter-of-fact tone. It wasn't my intention to ask so seriously, but in order to maintain control of the situation, my gut said, *This is no time to mess around.* "What are you laughing at?" I asked again to no one in particular. "Is somebody going to tell me what everyone finds so funny? I looked this stuff over earlier this morning, and I didn't find anything funny about it." (That, of course, was a lie. The only thing I accomplished before their arrival was catching up on some sleep.) After waiting a second or two for someone to say something, I decided to call on Amber Franklin. She looked like someone I could trust, even though she was clearly uncomfortable with the sudden attention.

"Um...you have...like, a mark on your forehead," she said squeamishly, as though she didn't want to hurt my feelings.

My face instantly burned with embarrassment remembering my recent catnap. This was not how I had intended to *capture their attention* or *blow their minds.*

Making our way through the lesson, I thought I was doing a decent job, but the atmosphere in the room said otherwise. It was still hot, and math was the last thing they wanted to do. I had made an effort to ask easy questions. The kind that didn't require a lot of energy. Nothing. Had their eyes not been blinking, my classroom looked more like a wax museum. "Come on," I said. "This is not that hard. For Pete's sake, this is stuff you did in fourth and fifth grade! Shall I send you all down the hall to Mrs. Denkins' class? Maybe she needs to review some of this stuff with you." If I was hoping for a little jumpstart, I didn't get it. I hadn't even finished what I was saying, and I noticed about eight kids looking up at the clock.

"What time is lunch?" asked Peter Hedler, one of the largest boys in class. He sat slouched in his chair with his huge feet sticking out into the aisle way.

"The same time it was yesterday," I retorted. *Boy, Gretchen would be so proud of me.* "I'm not going to tell you guys what time lunch is every day. Besides, the bell isn't what dismisses you. I do. The bell only serves as my reminder, but you're not going to lunch until I say so. And judging by the amount of effort this class is putting into math right now, we're probably going to be late."

Francene Milson piped up from the back row, "I forgot too. What time is lunch again?" I just stared at the back wall. Dumbfounded.

Incredible, I thought. These kids are more interested in knowing what time lunch is served than doing math. "11:45!" I yelled. "It was 11:45 yesterday, it's 11:45 today, and it's going to be 11:45 from here on out. Got it? Now don't ask again!" Scanning the crowd, there was a wide variety of reactions. Some of them looked scared, some looked confused, and a few others had a look of complete satisfaction on their little mugs.

Trying to carry on with the lesson, I told them I didn't want to hear any talking unless it was accompanied by a raised hand. Immediately, three boys raised their hands and started talking at once. "Do you want to stay in during lunch and work on this?" I asked. Smiling, they shook their heads in a horizontal direction, signaling they weren't interested.

The back of the room was starting to get very restless. Their interest in me wasn't very lofty to begin with, and their attention spans were depleting by the minute. "I don't feel too good," came a tiny voice from the left side of the room. It belonged to Rudy Teigan, one the smaller boys in class. He looked like a third-grader, and I had noticed he was a very busy boy. I was ready for this, having tried this trick many times myself as a student. Getting teachers to excuse students from class for any reason at all, especially being sick, has been around since the beginning of time. It did feel a little strange to be on the other side of it, though. Thinking on my feet was a strength yet to be developed, and I needed to make a quick decision. If I made him stay, and he actually was sick, there's a good chance my room was going to smell like puke for a few days. Of course, if he was allowed to leave, who knows what kind of mischief he could be causing in the hallway or bathroom.

"What's wrong?" I asked in an agitated way.

"I think I'm going to throw up," he said weakly.

"Well, I don't want that junk on the carpet," I snapped. "You better get outta here...and take the trash can with you. I don't think

Frank wants that stuff stinking up the hallway, either." Something told me this kid was lying, and I was going to be ready for him when he got back.

Taking up the math lesson and trying to concern myself with Rudy was kind of tricky. Trying to do one thing well was difficult enough.

After a few minutes he returned. Seeing him walk back in the room, I quickly walked over towards him and directed him back out into the hallway. Once we were both out there, I got down real close and said, "Now Rudy, I know you're probably not sick. I want you to open your mouth. I'm going to smell your breath." Big mistake. He had in fact thrown up. The intensity of stomach acid on his breath just about knocked me backwards. Lesson learned.

During lunch that afternoon, I quickly gulped down my food and headed for the only place a guy can truly find peace and quiet. The bathroom. With the shortage of men in the building, it was a pretty safe bet no one would be bothering me. Pushing open the large wooden door, I walked over to the stall and went in, locking the door behind me. The typical chatter in the teachers' lounge didn't seem appealing. Sitting there with my head in my hands, staring at the floor, I tried to gather my thoughts for the afternoon. I needed a game plan, something other than me doing a lot of talking and my students pretending to listen. To some, holding their pencil between their index finger and thumb and then bouncing it in the air, making it look like it was made of rubber, was a hundred times more interesting than listening to me. Maybe I could bounce around and make myself look like I was made of rubber while I taught social studies this afternoon.

Sitting there in the quiet, I didn't even notice the door opening in the stall next to me and the presence of another person until I was done envisioning myself as *rubber man*. Looking down, an enormous pair of white orthopedic shoes settled in on my left. The kind old ladies wear. "What in the world..." I started to say. *You've got to be kidding me. What is Joyce Rinker doing in here?!?! This is the men's bathroom!* She was the only person around here with feet that big. The lunch lady was sitting next to me...*in the bathroom!*

Without thinking, I grabbed my tie and shoved it in my mouth to keep from laughing out loud. I slid my shoes to the right, praying she hadn't seen me, and that's when things got worse. "Sure is hot out there today," she said. The only thing I could think to say was, "Mmm," in a quiet voice. Looking through the tiny crack between the divider, I tried to determine who was in the wrong room. Not seeing a urinal, I quickly stood up and bolted through the door. I practically ran back to my room, hoping to cleanse myself of the awful experience. Feeling my forehead, tiny drops of sweat trickled down the side of my face. Wiping them away, I couldn't imagine things getting any worse. Boy, was I wrong.

"What are we going to do now?" Camille Sniderson, who happened to be one of the more vocal girls in class, asked as they returned from lunch. "We don't have to do social studies, do we?"

I never would have thought of walking into my classroom as a student and asking my teacher that question. These kids have some nerve. "Yes, we're going to do social studies," I told her. "If you want to keep asking with that whiny tone in your voice, you're going to end up doing social studies all afternoon."

That seemed to work. She rolled her eyes and shuffled back to her desk.

The next few days proved to be very difficult. The warm weather was still hanging around. One of the more intense moments centered on a bee buzzing around the room after coming through a hole in the screen. Kids were screaming and running all over the room. "You know, class," I voiced over the commotion, "most bees go right for the loudest object!" There wasn't any science backing up my claim, but a couple of the kids calmed down somewhat. After several minutes, some of them were still riled up, forcing me to talk louder than I wanted. "Sit down!" I yelled. It was taking a lot of energy trying to keep this class from turning into full-fledged bedlam.

About ten minutes later, Frank walked by the window outside with an enormous leaf blower strapped to his back. Not only did the sound increase every time he pinched the throttle, but it also kicked up such a cloud of dust and debris that my classroom began to look a little murky. Not one kid in my class was looking in my direction. It was so loud I couldn't even hear myself. Looking out the window at Frank, the smile on his face was a pretty good indicator that he was enjoying himself and knew exactly what was going on.

Late one morning, as we were walking down the hallway to lunch, Bryan Brookens, as usual, was stirring up trouble. A cloud of commotion seemed to follow him wherever he went. "Get back to the room," I snapped. "If you can't walk quietly, go back to the room and sit down. I'll be back to get you in five minutes." He wasn't the only one goofing around, but he was the most obvious one. This kid had a bulls-eye on his back that was getting bigger every day.

"I didn't do anything!" he shouted back. "Why do you always yell at me?"

By this time the rest of the class had slowed down; some had stopped altogether. I shot back, "Because you're always in the middle of the action. Get back to the room, now!"

It wasn't until I finished my own lunch that I remembered sending him back to the room. Quickly getting up out of my seat, I practically ran down the hallway. Feelings of anger and frustration, along with some guilt for having left him alone in the room unsupervised, coursed through my body. Arriving at the door, I noticed the room was completely empty. "That little…" I started to say, but I was so upset, I couldn't even think straight.

My vision of what things were supposed to be like was vanishing like a desert mirage. It seemed the harder I clamped down, the more they resisted. By the end of the fourth week, I was emotionally exhausted. Doubts of whether I had chosen the right profession were creeping through my mind like a stalking cat. The apathy emitted by these kids was sickening. In my innermost parts, I felt the need to do something drastic. Perhaps throwing a pencil across the room or maybe taking my chair and flipping it over would get their attention, but I knew I hadn't been teaching long enough to get away with doing something like that.

I sort of chuckled to myself, thinking about the times I used to sit in my seat as a student, watching one of my teachers get frazzled.

When I was in eighth grade, the class objective was to get Mrs. Feely, our teacher, to really lose her cool. She was straight out of Gary Larson's *The Far Side*. Her slumped, overweight body was like a pear with arms. A pear full of dynamite. The sooner we could get her to scream and yell at us, the sooner we could really start to enjoy our time in school. It turned into a competition between the classes forced to sit through her sessions. The record for the previous year's class was 11:27 a.m. The year before that, she had stood on top of her desk and yelled obscenities at exactly 11:32 a.m. The record was 10:47 a.m., set by a class in 1975, one of the most dysfunctional classes ever assembled in Coleman. Their combination of low IQ's, poor attitudes, and inabilities to pay attention has caused them to live on in the annals of school history. As legend has it, their fooling around caused her to climb to the top of her desk and start giving the class a piece of her mind. "If you kids don't shut up, I'm going to kick you all outta here," she would yell. Which was exactly what they wanted. *Get us away from this delusional psychopath!*

There was a drought in desk ascension from 1983-1986 because she had to be admitted to the nut house. Union involvement got her reinstated for the fall 1987, and she continued to teach until her retirement ten years later. Advancements in prescription drugs had raised the degree of difficulty in the competition for the later years, causing scores of students to miss out on one heck of a show.

I used to think it was funny until I found myself wanting to do the same thing. I don't know how people expect teachers to teach when there's so much garbage that we have to put up with. Teaching is one thing; managing a classroom is a whole different matter. If kids would sit and listen like they're supposed to, teaching would be a lot more enjoyable.

When Bryan came back after lunch, I gave him a lengthy glare. To make him feel bad, of course. What I really wanted to do was take him out in the hallway and give him a piece of my mind, but I knew because I had failed to follow through by going back to the room after five minutes, I had no grounds for getting in his face. For all I knew, he may have gone back to the room and waited. Probably not, though.

Several weeks later, I really let my students have it. "Class," I said as they were returning from lunch one afternoon, "there's going to be a few changes around here. First of all, I'm fed up with the lack of respect I'm getting from most of you." I started calmly, but my emotions started to get the best of me, and I went off script. "I wish some of you would just stay home if all you're going to do is disrupt my class. There are some in here who would like to learn." Though looking around, I would have been lucky to find anybody to fit that description. "I am sick and tired of coming in here and busting my hump for nothing," I told them. "I'm a heckuva lot older than you, and I'm certainly a lot smarter than all of you. If anyone thinks they're smarter than me, be my guest; you can take these books and plan the lessons. Why bother coming if you're only intent is to make my life miserable?" I paused for dramatic effect. I was a little surprised at what I was saying and even more surprised I didn't stop there. "When you come into this class, you need to sit down and start working on the assignment in front of you. How hard is that? We are wasting way too much time. If there's anyone who can't handle that responsibility, they will find themselves spending some quality time in the principal's office." By this time, the collar of my shirt began getting really tight, due to the pressure of my jugular vein pressing against it.

Walking around the room, I looked right at those kids who were giving me the most grief. Bryan Brookens got a lot of my attention.

As I wound down my ranting, I walked right into some bad air. One of the most noxious fumes known to mankind had enveloped the classroom like an invisible cloud of funkified air. It was the equivalent of getting slammed face first into a brick wall. *What do these kids eat?* Most of the class was either laughing or blaming someone, while a few kids pulled their shirts up over their noses. It was tempting to have them write, "I will not toot in class or laugh when someone does," but that seemed like it might be counterproductive. "Open your math books and start working!" I yelled. This class was driving me nuts.

Two days later, I returned to my room after lunch to find everything that had once been setting on my desk before lunch now in a jumbled pile of books, papers, and writing utensils scattered all over the floor. "Whoever did this is going to pay dearly," I said once they settled down and took their seats. "No one is leaving until I find out who did this." I looked at them sternly, glaring right at my prime suspects. "I hope some of you don't mind walking home," I said threateningly, "because that's exactly what's going to happen if nobody fesses up." Slowly bending over, I managed to pick up the papers and knick-knacks that had earlier adorned my desk. Returning my angry stare back to the class, I noticed a small girl towards the back of the room crying. It was Ann Rosenthal, a very tiny girl that I wasn't sure I'd even heard say anything out loud yet. "What's your problem?" I shouted. As soon as the words came out of my mouth, I knew it was wrong. But because I didn't want to appear weak, I kept looking at her. She slowly put her head down and wrapped her arms around her head just like she was getting ready to play Heads-Up-Seven-Up, except she didn't have her thumb sticking out for someone to press down. Her frail little body began producing tiny convulsions as she tried to keep her meltdown from garnering the attention of everyone else in the room.

Despite my earlier threat, the class left on time, without anyone coming forward. Trying to intimidate my class with hollow words that I knew I could never enforce left me feeling less than empty. Emotionally, my tank was dry as a bone. These kids had robbed me of the joy I thought teaching would bring. I hated this class of numbskulls, and from now on, they were going to pay for the trouble they were causing. It's too bad, too, because I like to consider myself a pretty nice guy. Too bad they kept acting like idiots. Oh well, it's their choice.

Later that evening after supper, the phone rang. When you live at home with your parents, there's an expectation that the phone is never for you. That's why I was surprised when my mom handed me the phone. "Hello," I said casually.

"Hi, Mr. Carter," a soft-spoken voice on the other end said. "This is Gene Rosenthal. My daughter Ann is in your class. I'm sorry to bug you at home, but Ann came home from school today a little upset, and I was wondering if you knew why."

That little ..., I thought to myself. "Uh...," I was drawing a blank. "What did she say?" I asked.

"Well, she got off the bus this afternoon, and her eyes were all red like she'd been crying. When I asked her what was wrong, she started bawling. The only thing she said so far was that she hated school. Her mother and I were wondering if something happened at school today that would have caused her to be so upset."

"Well, I don't know for sure," came my answer. "Maybe something happened on the playground during recess." My guts were churning. I knew full well why their daughter was crying, and I'd just lied right to her father. "I'll keep an eye on things at school," I continued. "If I have an opportunity to talk with her tomorrow, I'll follow up on things."

"We appreciate that, Mr. Carter. She's always loved school, so her mom and I were quite surprised when she got off the bus today so disturbed." Hanging up the phone, I felt sick to my stomach. I don't know what it feels like to get shot in the stomach with a twelve-gauge shot gun at point blank range, but I imagined this was close. I had no intention of asking Ann why she was crying. I didn't have to, because I already knew. My unprofessional, irritable behavior was making nice kids like Ann hate school and, more than likely, hate me.

Lying in bed that night, before drifting off to sleep, I questioned myself and what I was doing. Questions like *Why on earth did I pick this line of work?* and *Is this really what the next thirty years are going to be like?* kept tumbling around my brain like a load of wet laundry.

Later that week, after assigning an extremely heavy load of work to get them to be quiet, I decided to try and actually teach something to these kids again. It was time for social studies, a subject I had learned within a very short period was not their favorite. The increase of yawning, asking to go to the bathroom, and note-writing were dead giveaways. There were some moans and rolling of the eyes after telling them to take out their textbooks, but I didn't care. "If I hear any more negative sounds coming from this class,

I'm going to double your assignment." Instant quiet. Finally, I was getting through to these boneheads. They had been reading about the exploration of the New World with names like La Salle, De Soto, and Columbus in heavy rotation.

Turning around to pull down the map, the ring attached to the wooden dowel at the base of the map was not within my grasp. In a moment of haste, I stood on my tip-toes and made a reach for the map. No luck. Instead of a graceful snatch, I looked more like a toddler trying to grab a plate of cookies off the kitchen counter. In my effort to seize the metal ring, my shirt slid up out of my pants, revealing more of me than they probably wanted to see. Grabbing a chair from the side table, I made a mental note to put some string on the handle, so I wouldn't have to emphasize my shortness every time I wanted to use the map.

Stretching the map to its desired length, so all seven continents were visible, proved to be more difficult than originally expected. Loosening my grip on the map and sensing it was not going to stay in place, I jerked it quickly up and down with little to no effect. Squatting down to talk some sense into this cheap roll of plastic, I detected a feeling of satisfaction from my class as they watched me struggle at the front of the room. Finally, after several minutes of yanking on it, it stayed in place.

To see how well they had been reading the assignment, I asked, "What continent are all these explorers from?" Silence. "What did your book say? Do you guys need to read this again?" I ended up answering the question myself. "Europe," I said. "All these guys came from Europe." To emphasize my point, I pointed at Europe on the map. "Right here. Europe is right here."

As I touched the map, it rolled up so quickly that I barely managed to get my hand out of the way. SLAM!!!!! It clanked against the metal piece attaching it to the board so loudly my heart skipped a beat. Roars of laughter instantly filled the room. One kid was suppressing his laughter so much a huge snot bubble flared out his nostril. That made the class laugh even harder. My day was turning into a nightmare. The dreams people have of going to school or church in their underwear were nothing compared to this.

"Is this really that funny?" I asked, scowling at them in disgust. "Let's see how funny you think this is...read the next two chapters on your own and answer *all* the questions. Even the Critical Thinking ones!!"

They hated those questions more than anything. Just in case they forgot who was in charge around here, I had ways of reminding them.

Later that afternoon, I ran off several copies of meaningless worksheets to fill their time. While they go by a variety of names, they serve primarily one purpose: shutting students' mouths and using the energy that would have been spent disrupting class by filling in a bunch of blank spaces with their yellow number twos. I was desperately craving some peace and quiet, and this was the only way I knew how to get it. Except for the occasional sharpening of their writing instruments, there was nothing but the sound of pencils scraping paper for almost two hours. Once in a while, I'd get up from my desk and walk around the room to assure them I hadn't slipped into a coma. I took great pleasure in standing right behind some of my least favorite students—just to make them feel awkward.

I thought everything was great until I looked at the pile of papers on my desk at the end of the day. There were six stacks of papers. Each stack contained twenty-seven sheets. At the time, I thought I was being clever by making the worksheets back to back. I realized the price tag of a totally silent afternoon: a tremendous amount of papers that needed to be corrected. I wasn't in the mood to do a math problem, but it dawned on me that most of my evening would consist of sitting at the dining room table, correcting papers. The thought of giving them all A's or putting their work in the trash did cross my mind, though.

This class was so confusing. So unpredictable. They just couldn't put together a great day from beginning to end, even though there were times when they seemed willing to cooperate—though never for more than an hour or two. Just when things seemed to be going all right, some smart-aleck kid would say something like, "Hey, Mr. C, I noticed that you wear that shirt a lot. Is it your favorite one?"

He would manage to get through most of it before busting out laughing. It was like a game. One of his buddies had probably dared him to ask the question. Sure enough, several snorts and chuckles were heard throughout the room. My face burned.

Usually I tried to ignore them, but occasionally I would let one of them have it. "You think you're funny?" I'd say with my eyes boring an imaginary hole into his forehead. "Let's see how funny you think it is when I call your parents tonight."

They knew I wouldn't call. What was I going to say? "Excuse me, Mr. So-and-so, do you know what your son said to me at school today? He asked me if I was wearing my favorite shirt." Just thinking about a conversation like that seemed a little weird. Almost like I was tattling.

I remember thinking how nice it was to be free of Larry's Lumber after working there so many hot, muggy summers in high school. Nothing against manual labor, but having sweat cascade down your body while loading and unloading lumber, or worse yet, while throwing rolls of pink insulation up to the second floor of a metal-sided pole barn with temperatures hovering in the high eighties or low nineties wasn't something I felt like doing for forty years. After today, though, I wasn't so sure.

Standing in front of those kids every day was like getting thrown to the wolves. Maybe a little sweat on my brow wouldn't be so bad after all. At least if I worked at Larry's, there'd be no worries about twelve and thirteen-year-olds getting their kicks from watching me get frustrated and annoyed. My class had made a game out of getting me riled up, and so far the score was about seventy-eight to zero. It's kind of tough to score when you're always playing defense.

Chapter 6

Party Time

O ctober has always been one of my favorite months. Despite having thirty-one days, it always seems to be the shortest. Chilly mornings. Bright blue skies. The abundant maples, with their varying colors of red, yellow, and orange leaves, have always left me feeling content. There's a sort of peace that goes along with autumn. In a word, it's perfect. Too bad it doesn't last longer than a couple of weeks. The discouraging part was that all this colorful scenery would be replaced by varying shades of brown and gray in late November and December.

For many of us in northern Michigan, autumn is the time to get ready for winter, which for some includes stacking wood in rows long and high enough to last several months, as it's not uncommon to still have cold weather and snow deep into April.

My family was no exception. Growing up, we all had our different roles in the wood gathering process. My dad was the only one allowed to use the chainsaw. My brother and I were responsible to load the newly sectioned logs into the back of our old Ford pickup. Every time we got into the woods and out of the truck, my father would remind us, "Whatever you do, don't knock out the back window." This wasn't my ideal way of spending a Saturday morning, but one I knew was necessary.

It was the same thing every time we cut wood: a quiet drive

with my brother on the far right, near the window, and me in the middle, sandwiched between the two. My dad wasn't much of a talker, especially when it came to my brother and me. The conversation tended to stay on the surface. My dad's way of thanking us for our labor was to buy us a bottle of Orange Crush and a small bag of potato chips for my brother and me to share. Thad always took the first half, therefore leaving me with a bottle of lukewarm soda with tiny bits of potato chips mixed in.

We'd burned wood ever since I could remember. My dad liked the heat. "You can't beat wood heat," he always said. "The only fuel that warms you twice." He meant a person usually stayed warm while cutting and stacking it as well as when using it in the wood stove to heat the house.

The wood stove was down in the basement, but I never remember my dad actually putting wood in it. Perhaps that's why he had my brother and me. Two servants to do the odd jobs he didn't feel like doing. I didn't mind loading up the wood stove during the day, but my heart sank to my ankles whenever I had to do it at night. When I was in third grade, I read a book that had vivid details involving demons, and I distinctly remember seeing a picture of Satan in the book. My overactive imagination put Satan in the basement. Sometimes he would hide under the stairs and try to grab my ankles and yank me into hell. Other times, he would hide in the well pit and just try to scare me. I'd creep down the stairs as slow as I could, hoping that if I was quiet enough, he wouldn't hear me. I'd slide my stocking'd feet along the wooden slabs that served as our steps. One hand on the railing. My theory: Keep a tight grip on the banister, which was wobbly to begin with, and if someone or something did grab my ankles and try to drag me through the steps, the railing would likely pop off the wall and keep me from getting pulled through. It felt like I was down there for an hour, but it was probably only a minute or two. Slowly, I'd open the door to the wood stove, tip-toe to the rows of stacked wood, and quietly, gently take a piece or two off the pile. I was saving all my energy for the return trip. It was exactly three steps back to the stairs, and as soon as my foot touched the bottom stair, I was gone like a speeding

bullet through the barrel of a gun. I turned into Jesse Owens sprinting for the finish line. Every time, I'd return to the living room out
of breath. "What's going on down there?" my mom or dad would
ask. My reply? "Nothing." I still have a scar on my right shin from
the time I slipped. Even now as an adult, I tend to go upstairs a little
faster than I go down, making sure my feet are firmly planted on
each step.

When I was younger, late September and early October was
also a time for my family to help some of the area fruit farmers by
picking apples. That was another form of labor I wasn't particu-
larly fond of, but the extra money was always useful. Sometimes
it helped buy jackets or other miscellaneous things we needed for
the oncoming winter. Thad and I had the job of picking the apples
that had fallen off the tree onto the ground, referred to as *drops*.
Using our five-gallon buckets, we'd drop them in two or three at
a time until it was full. The next step involved carrying or—in my
case—dragging the bucket to a large crate, hoisting it up over the
edge, and letting the apples cascade into the emptiness below. Half
our time was spent working on our assigned task, the other half was
spent trying to hit each other in the head with rotten apples. Once
Thad and I were older and became more involved in school and
sports, this fall custom fell by the wayside.

Getting older, the silence between my dad and me seemed a
little more awkward, especially during my teenage years. It would
have been nice to talk about something that mattered. When I was
thirteen or fourteen, I remember being very nervous whenever he
and I were alone, afraid he would attempt to tell me about the
birds and the bees. Looking back, I had nothing to worry about; a
man who tends to stay on the surface would never dare bring up
that subject. I always wondered about the other boys in my school.
Had their fathers discussed these things with them? What if my dad
never told me? Would I be able to figure it out myself? So many
questions. Questions that turned to fear. Fear that I might be the
only one who didn't know what to do when the opportunity arose.
I'd never marry. I'd be in my thirties or forties and someone might
ask, "Are you married yet?" "No, " I'd say. "Haven't found the

right one yet." All the while it was really because *I didn't know*.

Besides the beauty of the season, another reason I was so excited for autumn this year in particular was the "killing frost." The cold, frosty mornings were a welcome relief from the unusually warm summer we had just experienced. I was tired of trying to compete for the students' attention with the buzzing insects that seemed to find all the holes in the window screen despite the Scotch tape used to cover many of them up. The cooler temperatures also meant I could wear long sleeves and possibly even a sweater to help hide the sweat stains. The awful smell that accompanied many of the boys was gone too. For some reason, boys at this age tend to keep their distance from baths and showers. Deodorant is pretty much out of the picture as well. Many times these boys would come in from recess in the afternoon surrounded by this horrible funk, similar to older ladies who wear way too much cheap perfume. The ones who announce their arrival a minute or two before they *actually arrive...* with their aroma. These boys, on the other hand, smell nothing like perfume. It was more a combination of wet dog and bacon grease.

I wish my thoughts about teaching matched the beautiful weather outside, but they didn't. I knew I was losing ground with my students. Instead of capturing their minds, I'd created and magnified a climate of fear and apathy. I had no clout with these kids, and I wondered if I'd made a huge mistake in going into this profession. What amazed me most was that I was turning into so many of the teachers who had caused me to be fearful and simply *not care* about anything closely resembling education as a kid.

I did have one teacher in high school whom I liked. I remember really enjoying his class. *It was math, for Pete's sake!* I hated math, but I loved Mr. Fritz. I would have laid down my life for him. Instead of laying down their lives for me, I had a feeling my students would probably rather *take* mine.

If I wasn't fighting with my class for their attention, I was usually engaged in battle with the clock. There were times when the clock seemed to stop. It was as though the clock were a living, breathing life form, knowing just when to slow down and when to speed up—at seemingly the worst times.

The days melted into weeks, and I was not feeling at all like the kind of teacher I had hoped to become. Sitting in my room before the kids came in was the only time I felt any sort of peace. In a short time, those knuckle-heads would be walking in, trying to make my life miserable. I just didn't get it. Didn't these kids know that if they didn't get good grades and get into a good college, they were going to end up living a dead end life?

One Wednesday afternoon in late October, I was wading my way through another math lesson. I had recently begun to notice several students asking to use the bathroom during math, and I was beginning to get annoyed by it. If I didn't allow them to use the bathroom and someone wet their pants or got a bladder infection, I'd never hear the end of it. On the other hand, I was almost certain most of them didn't really have to go all that bad.

Bryan Brookens raised his hand shortly into the lesson. "I gotta take a leak," he said with a smirk on his face.

The class went silent as they waited to see how I would respond. Nothing clever came to me, so I just stared at him for about ten seconds, wishing I could wring his little neck.

"Hurry up," I said finally, staring down at him. Nothing says, "I mean business," like a good stare. Again, I tried to continue with the math lesson. After showing them what to do, I gave them a few problems to try on their own. "Okay, let's take a look at problem number one," I said. "Who's got the answer?"

Pete Hedler raised his hand slowly. "Yes, Pete. What did you get?"

"Can I go to the bathroom?" My body temperature instantly went from 98.6 to 110 degrees.

"NO!!!" I yelled. "No one's going to the bathroom until we finish this lesson. I have had it with everyone asking to use the bathroom." I prayed no one *really* had to go, but I was sick and tired of this nonsense. "Finish the problems on your own," I told them. "If you really have to use the bathroom, you may use it when you've finished all the problems. So…if you really have to go, you better get moving."

About ten minutes later, Bryan Brookens came strolling back

into the room. "Where have you been?" I asked, a little louder than intended.

"I had to take a dump. Geez, get off my back." Roars of laughter filled the room. Even the good kids who never got in trouble thought this was funny.

"Get in the hall!" I screamed. He slowly walked over to his desk, picked up his math book, and shuffled out into the hallway. Getting kicked out of class was a small price to pay for the amusement he provided the class. It was clear this kid thrived on attention, regardless of the form it took.

As everyone knows, the last day of October is Halloween. As a child, it was my chance to dress-up, pretend to be someone or something else, and more importantly, get as much candy as humanly possible in a few short hours. My most bountiful year of accumulating loot happened in fifth grade. Clip and I made out like bandits. We had so much candy that we both got sick of eating it and actually sold most of it to our classmates well into late November. Every time I eat—or even smell—chocolate, it takes me right back to that night. Earlier that day, we had taken two brand new bed sheets from his mom's linen closet. They were still in the plastic packaging. His mom was not happy when she found out, which cost both of us four candy bars to make things right. In addition to being beige-colored ghosts, we also went around a second time as construction workers—having taken some tools and other instrument-like doodads from our fathers.

As a teacher, Halloween takes on a whole different meaning. It went from being something I used to anticipate to something I dreaded. As the kids walked in that day, I could feel the tension in the air. These kids were wound tighter than a guitar string. Trying to get and hold their attention was becoming more and more difficult with every slow-sweep of the minute hand. Six boys already had their faces painted like vampires. Two girls came in wearing see-through fairy costumes, leaving little to the imagination.

"Go to the office, girls," I said. "There's no way you're wearing that in here." They both rolled their eyes and left in a huff.

By lunch, I had collected four sets of vampire teeth, two fake cigarettes, one pipe, three containers of white make-up, and six sword-like weapons. "You'll get these back in June," I said, knowing full well I wasn't planning to keep them that long. What kind of a cruel tyrant keeps kids' toys until June? I really wanted to, but knowing some of their parents would be here later in the afternoon to help at the party made me realize I didn't have the guts to follow through with it.

Time slowed to a mere crawl. By lunch, I felt like I had put in a full day with very little energy left for teaching. In science, we were reviewing for a quiz on the solar system. Towards the end of our session, Bryan raised his hand with a question. The huge smile on his face should have been a warning, but due to my exhausted state, I ignored it. He proceeded to ask me whether or not a certain planet had "rings." Before he even finished the question, roars of laughter erupted from my class. He had tried so hard not to laugh when he asked the question that he ended up spitting all over the girl in front of him. Total chaos.

"Go to the office!" I screamed. "Don't plan on being here for the party either."

Slowly, he rose up out of his chair and walked out of the room. As he left, the door slammed so hard that our solar-system mobiles hanging from the ceiling swayed back and forth for several seconds. I could only imagine what kind of hand gestures and body gyrations he was making in the hallway. *Who cares where he goes, as long he gets his sorry rear-end out of my room*, I thought.

As if the day wasn't stressful enough, the last hour and a half of school was totally devoted to a Halloween party, which was going to put me around their parents. I worried about the kind of stories these kids had been telling their parents about me.

The party was supposed to start at exactly 2:00 with an all-school parade. Because this was a new experience for me, I told my kids to start getting into their costumes at 1:30. Huge mistake. It took exactly twelve seconds for most of them to get ready, leaving twenty-nine minutes of pure pandemonium. Even the most mild-mannered children were running around like they had hot coals in their pants. Kids screaming. Boys engaged in sword fights that involved gouging each other and trying to cut the other person's head off with their plastic weapons. One kid took it upon himself to hide behind the door and try and scare everyone that walked through. The pinnacle of his success came as one of the classroom mothers came in carrying a tray of meat and cheese. As he jumped out, she dropped the whole thing.

Because I didn't want to make these parents think I was a total jerk, I struggled with the battle between stepping in and putting an end to this madness, or trying to look calm and hope things settled down on their own. Six seconds later, I realized things were not going in the right direction. "Everybody sit down!" I screamed. "Put your heads down, now!" When you've reached a point where you're telling your class to put their heads down, especially sixth-graders, you've lost the battle.

My classroom was quiet for about thirty-four seconds, until the other half of the class came back from changing their clothes. The half of the class that had missed my short tirade. Those minutes leading up to two o'clock were some of the most painful minutes I've ever had as a teacher.

After the parade, the time remaining was spent trying to eat and play games. I quickly learned that relay games are not appropriate for Halloween parties. Neither are games like *Pictionary* which involved a lot of screaming and yelling on the students' part.

A few minutes before dismissal, Pete Hedler walked up to me. There was a paleness to his face that had nothing to do with white make-up. "I think I'm gonna be—" Before he could finish, he spewed the contents of his stomach all over the floor, splattering in all directions.

"Somebody get Frank!" I yelled. Kids began running and screaming all around the room. "Peeuuuuu!" they all yelled. Most of the parents just stood around, holding the walls up, watching this train wreck unfold. Without hesitation, I said, "Okay, anyone who's riding a bus or walking home, you may leave now." I knew Boggins wouldn't appreciate me letting my class out early, but at this point, I didn't care. I felt like I'd been run over by a freight train pulling enough box cars to stretch a mile.

The only good thing about today was the paycheck sitting in my mailbox. A month ago, I'd noticed a new teller at the bank. She was kind of cute and didn't appear to have a wedding ring, either. Best of all, I didn't recognize her, meaning she probably wasn't from Coleman, which ultimately meant she wasn't familiar with me or any of my family. Scoping out potential women of interest had been turned up a few notches since living with mom and dad. Any likely prospect caused my heart to pitter-patter, allowing my mind to entertain thoughts of going on actual dates. Going out with anyone on Friday or Saturday night would be better than watching TV with my parents or sitting in the basement plucking my guitar.

In my mind, it was so easy. I'd mosey up to the counter, cash my check, and before turning around to leave, I'd say something witty. "What time do you get off work tonight?" I'd ask in a calm, cool sort of way. "Not soon enough," she'd reply back with an I-like-you-but-I'm-not-going-to-make-it-easy-for-you smile. "I'll be at Gretchen's, across the street. If you want to get together, that's where you'll find me." Then, as she counted my money back, she'd let her fingers fall delicately in the palm of my hand, causing spasms of warm fuzzies to shoot through my chest and into my outer extremities. Her soft, warm hand would linger just a little too long, and as she slid her index finger across my palm, we could both feel the magical warmth of unbridled passion that was screaming inside our bodies.

Finally walking into the bank, my palms were sweating like crazy with the exciting possibility of talking to an attractive girl. Looking toward the counter, I saw her, but unfortunately the object of my affection was helping another customer.

"Can I help you?" came a small, soft voice. It was Mary Dexter. A woman who had worked at Coleman State Bank since the Depression. Decision time. Refuse Mary's offer and appear rude to possibly take advantage of getting some attention from a girl I desperately wanted to notice me? In the name of passivity, I shuffled forward and handed Mary my check. "What are we going to do today?" she asked.

"Put it all in savings, except for sixty bucks," I told her, signing the back of my check with the provided pen. I glanced to my left. The current object of my affection was talking to Russ Bradley, a guy who had graduated a year behind me. He was good-looking *and* charming, which meant there'd be no afternoon rendezvous at Gretchen's for me and the mystery girl today. She was laughing a little too much. It was clear from the body language there wasn't any banking being done between the two. Never a good sign for guys on the outside.

"See you tonight," he said, turning around.

Ouch! My insides instantly went flat. My diaphragm slowly deflated like an old basketball.

"Looking forward to it," she said, smiling back at him.

Taking my sixty bucks and walking back out to my car, I felt dejected. For the second time today, I felt like a total and complete loser. Every time I started to get excited and zero in on someone, it never turned out.

The thought of calling one of those matchmaking services was becoming more and more appealing all the time. *Only losers do that sort of thing,* I thought to myself. With my luck, I'd end up going on a date with the bearded lady from Barnum & Bailey. Of course, we'd both be so desperate that it wouldn't matter.

After supper, I went straight to bed. At some point during the night, I dreamed I was in a car with someone else. I couldn't see the other person very well, but I was certain it was a girl. Her laughter sounded familiar. Catching a glimpse of her out of my peripheral vision, it looked as though it might be the girl from the bank. Yes! It was the girl from the bank. Her soft, delicate hand was firmly clasped in mine. Sure, my hands were sweating, but it didn't seem to bother her. I turned to look at her. What was happening? Was she leaning in for a kiss? She was! She was! She stopped short. What was going on? Looking down, I realized why she was laughing. *I was in my underwear!* It wasn't just any underwear. It was my dad's underwear! The white Fruit of the Looms with a blue and gold striped waistband. They were way too big, forcing me to pinch my legs together. They were extremely thin, too, like wearing tissue paper. I didn't dare move for fear of tearing them. As dreams often go, there's no rhyme or reason for what happens. One minute you're in a car, and the next second you're somewhere else. It began to dawn on me that I was at school for some reason. To get money from my desk, maybe. Yes, to get money from my desk so I could buy some pants. The next thing I knew, I was floating above my body with a bird's eye view of the whole situation. Not only was I wearing my dad's underwear, but I was also wearing blue dress socks pulled up to my kneecaps. Underwear and dress socks! The last thing I remembered from my dream was hiding in the bathroom. I had gone into one of the stalls and stood on top of the toilet so the kids couldn't see my feet, but somehow they knew I was in there. I looked under the divider between the stalls and saw Gus Harble wearing a sport coat and light blue boxer shorts standing on the toilet next to me. I could hear kids coming in, banging on the stall doors. Kids were getting down on their hands and knees looking under the doors. Boys...*and girls!* Laughing hysterically at the two of us. When I woke up, my pillow was soaked with sweat. I'd just experienced a nightmare of the worst kind. Looking over at my alarm clock, it read 3:54 a.m. I felt my entire body flush with relief, realizing I had just been dreaming. Trying to rid my mind of Gus in the bathroom was going to be my homework for the weekend.

CHAPTER 7

Burn Out

"State standardized testing starts next Monday," Boggins told me as he entered my room late one week. "Our scores haven't been all that great for some time now. No pressure, but we have to get these scores up, or the state will take over our school." I'd totally forgotten about the MEAT test, *Michigan Educational Assessment Testing*. For years people always wondered what genius came up with that title. Not only was the acronym kind of silly, it seemed pointless to say *assessment* and *testing* in the same breath. Aren't they pretty much the same thing?

There's no shortage of acronyms in the teaching profession. There are titles and labels for everything. Instead of being strong-willed, it's Oppositional Defiant Disorder (O.D.D). Attention issues...A.D.D. Can't speak English? Then you're ESL. Got emotional issues? That makes you E.I. The list goes on.

"What does that mean?" I asked, referring to his statement about state takeover.

"It means they will control every facet of our instructional day," he replied matter-of-factly.

"What impact will that have on me?"

"It means the state will come in here and tell us exactly what to teach, when to teach it, and how to teach it." That didn't sound too bad to me.

"What's so bad about that?" I inquired.

"Well, the absolute truth is…the state prints these scores in the newspaper, and I'm tired of being at the bottom of the list. Do you know how embarrassing it is to be swimming at the bottom of the educational fish tank year after year?"

It wasn't clear whether he wanted these kids to improve for their sake or if he was only concerned with making himself look good.

Later that afternoon, I walked down the hall to Gus Harble's classroom to see what his plan was for giving these state tests in the areas of reading, writing, and math. Maybe he had some knowledge he'd be willing to share. Right before I got to his door, I had to stop and compose myself as my mind drifted back to my recent dream. He' s been teaching in Coleman for over thirty years, and I figured he'd be my best shot at figuring out what to do. There's a name for guys like Harble: *Dinosaur.* There's a small part of me that thinks he just came up out of the ground one day as an old man and got a teaching job in the closest town to the crack in the earth he came up out of.

I knew it was going to be a little awkward, because he had been my seventh grade teacher. I wasn't sure if I should call him Mr. Harble or Gus. Worse than that was the fact that Clip and I had once wrapped a package of breath mints in newspaper as a joke at Christmas. We put it on his desk when he wasn't looking and were hoping to make it out of there before we spotted them. Our stomachs sank to the floor as we watched him briskly walk over to his desk to check out the mystery item. His face went from slight happiness at the thought that someone actually thought of him and bought him a present, to one of anger in a matter of seconds. "What's this supposed to mean?" he irritably asked the whole class, holding the package of mints for everyone to see. Though he threatened to keep us until someone fessed up, it ended up being only five minutes after the bell because legally he had to let us go. He ended his tirade by saying, "I can see why some animals eat their young." Despite not getting caught, several days of watching us like a hawk proved Clip and I were the prime suspects. Now, walking into his room to ask for advice was a bit uncomfortable, to say the least.

"Hey, Mr. Harble," I said, strolling through the doorway into his room. His classroom was set up in traditional rows. There was one poster stuck on the wall. It had a picture of a basketball player, wearing a skin tight uniform, slam dunking a basketball. Written at the top in block lettering were the words: Give Your Best. It was the same poster that graced his wall when I had him, and it was old back then. It's hard to imagine that a poster could actually collect dust, but sure enough, as the light hit it just right, the layer of dust that had accumulated over the past thirty years became visible.

His legacy was to give lots of detentions. The rumor was he gave the detentions because *he* was the detention supervisor. If there weren't any kids for detention, he was out of an extra job that week, and his paycheck was a little lighter. As kids, we believed he got paid for each person in detention.

"Hey, Mr. Harble," I said again.

Without looking up from his desk, he said, "Call me Gus." *I knew I'd get it wrong.* At that point, I decided to refrain from call-ing him anything. It reminded me of my dad who never called my Grandma Jensen (my mom's mother) anything. It was kind of funny to watch him. He would just start talking to her if he needed to get her attention. We all knew he didn't want to call her *Mom,* and of course to call her Wanda would have been even more uncomfort-able. Then when we'd get in the car to drive home, it was always, "Your mom this…" and "Your mom that…" So there I was, finding myself in a situation paralleling that of my father with the same painful results.

"Hey, what do you know about these tests we're supposed to be giving next week?"

"Oh, the MEAT test," he replied, not looking up from the pa-pers he was correcting. "It starts next week. What do you want to know?"

"Well, I guess I'm really not sure what I'm supposed to do."

"Look, it's real easy," he said. "You hand out the tests. Give them about an hour or so to work on them. When they're done, they hand it in. That's all there is to it."

"It's just that I was talking with Boggins earlier today, and he said he really needed us to do well," I said. "Did he say anything to you about trying to get these kids to score better so we don't keep looking like we have the dumbest kids in the county every year?"

"Oh…he used to try get me fired-up, but I've got to be honest with you, Ted, I really don't care how these kids do. My paycheck is the same whether they all pass or all fail. I'll make this as simple as I can. The people in this town don't care about education. Every time we ask for more money to buy something or get a new piece of equipment, we get turned down. Don't you think if this community supported our schools, we'd do better? Therefore, I've decided *not* to care. It's just easier that way. If I get all fired-up and start ranting and raving, it's not going to do any good, anyway. Why get my underwear all wadded up for nothing?"

"Yeah, I suppose you're right," I said, although deep down I don't think I totally agreed with what he was saying. I had to make a decision as to whether this issue was more important than the relationship. That's tough; I didn't want to get on Gus' bad side, but I could also see that he wasn't going to be much help to me…ever. As a matter of fact, walking into his classroom sort of brought back some of the same feelings I had as a student in his class. This man was dull, boring, and lifeless. I'm sure I learned something from him, but having a skin graft would have been more enjoyable than listening to him drone on and on about whatever it was he talked about. My memories of being in his class consisted of either listening to his monotone rumbling or the stifling silence of seat work. Lots of it too. The volume rarely reached half capacity, and if it did, he was on us like stink on a monkey. Just the look on his face was enough to make most kids straighten up. However, there were always those two or three kids who felt it was their personal responsibility to see just exactly where the line in the sand had been drawn. If his "death stare" didn't cause things to improve, he'd get right in your face and accentuate every syllable of his spiel by jabbing his finger into your chest. Most of us could never really hear what he was saying to the offender, so we always tried to read his lips. I was pretty sure I heard him tell Clip he was going to "knock his head off if he didn't straighten up and fly right." We found out later that Harble just said, "You better knock it off and fly right." The only thing Clip remembered was that his breath smelled like mothballs and vinegar. Just the thought of someone's bad breath in my face was enough incentive to keep him off my back.

I walked out of his room feeling even more discouraged and confused than when I walked in. I could see his point, though. What difference did it make how the kids performed? It wasn't any skin off my chin if they failed miserably. Deep down in the pit of my gut, I knew I would have a greater sense of satisfaction if they *actually* did well, and I wanted them to do well, but given the current situation in my room, the forecast was likely they wouldn't.

The rest of the week crawled by at a snail's pace. I was almost positive there was an extra day in there somewhere. There's nothing worse than waking up on Thursday morning thinking it's Friday. It felt like Friday, and there's a part of me that tried to convince myself that it *actually* was Friday, but then I heard the garbage man go by, and I knew it was only Thursday.

Lying in bed, my motivation to get up and get moving was in the negative numbers. Feeling discouraged, anxious, and annoyed all at once have a way of keeping a guy down. At the last possible moment, I rolled out of bed and began the usual routine of breakfast, shower, iron shirt, and finally, make my lunch for the day. Turning the ignition in my car yielded absolutely nothing. Not even a *whirrrr-rr-rr-rr* or that clicking sound cars sometimes make when there's just enough juice left in the battery to run the dome light but not nearly enough to crank the engine over. Looking down at the pull-out knob for the headlights, I noticed it was pushed in all the way. Apparently I hadn't left the lights on. Since my father had already left for work, the only pair of jumper cables had gone with him. I slowly got out, slammed the door a little harder than usual, and asked my mom for a ride to school. I had done this same kind of thing when I was in high school. I'd miss the bus on purpose, mainly so I wouldn't have to share a seat with a second grader. But today, I really wasn't looking forward to getting dropped off at school by my mother.

"Sure, I can give you a ride," she replied after I humbly asked her to take me to school.

"Thanks, but I need to leave soon."

"No problem. Just let me finish getting ready."

I knew that meant at least another fifteen minutes. I've never really figured out why it takes her so long to get ready in the morning. My father, on the other hand, takes roughly forty-five seconds to get ready as he does virtually nothing. His toothbrush, which is several years old, still looks brand new.

I could tell my mother was trying to hurry. When she walked out of the bathroom, she only had eyeliner on one eye and her earrings didn't match. I couldn't risk being any later than I already was, so I quietly hoped someone else would tell her.

As we got closer to school, I started to get very anxious. The thought of one of my students seeing me get dropped off by my mother was more than I could stand. "I'll walk," I said, just as the school was coming into view.

"No, no, no," she said. "You don't need to get out here and walk. I'm plenty early for work."

"No," I said a little more emphatically. "You are going to stop right here, and I'm going to get out." As soon as the words left my mouth, remorse filled the empty spaces in my stomach. The happiness on her face was now replaced with hurt. "I'm sorry," I said. "It's just that..." Sitting there stammering for words, nothing of great value seemed to rise up. "Sorry," I said one more time before getting out of the car. Without saying a word, she slowly drove off. Though I felt terrible, I knew she felt worse, which of course made me feel awful.

Later that morning in the middle of social studies, for no apparent reason, I realized that living with my parents was slowly driving a wedge in our already fragile relationship. After school, I called around to some apartments in the area but quickly found out living any place but home was not an option. While some of my friends from college were bringing down big bucks, I was not. Contrary to what many people think, I was not rolling in a six-figure salary. It was a meager five figure income, slightly higher than a manager at a fast food restaurant. Paying off my student loans left very little money for anything else.

That night, I popped the hood on my car and just stared. Because my mechanical skills are greatly lacking, opening the hood on a vehicle seemed like the most logical thing to do. Looking at the wires and tubes going here and there, I honestly couldn't tell the purpose of one thing from another. Some were different colors, while others were metal. I could tell that some were more important than others, but that's as far as it went. After looking at the car's engine for five minutes, I went back in the house to wait for my dad to finish watching the news. I knew better than to ask him during the highlight of his day. For whatever reason, my dad seems to function better when he knows who's been murdered in the big city and what the weather's going to be like for the next five days.

After the news, he slowly got out of his recliner and ambled out to the driveway where the car was parked. We took our places. He grabbed a few wrenches and other tools, while I went for the trouble-light. Even though I didn't know diddly-squat about cars, I could hold a light like it was nobody's business. I had perfected my craft with years and years of practice, getting to the point where I could almost anticipate where the light needed to be shone. And, what I'm the most proud of, I rarely blasted the high-intensity light in my dad's face anymore. He used to get so irked when I would accidentally shine it in his face. Not anymore, though. I was getting pretty good.

In his usual quiet way, he stood there looking at the contents of my motor. "You didn't leave the lights on, did you?"

Feeling rather proud of myself, I said, "No, I already checked that this morning."

He walked to the driver's side door, opened it, and sat down in the seat. Turning the key, he got the same results I had gotten earlier. Nothing. Almost as though he didn't believe what I'd said, he checked the pull-out knob for the headlights. Then he slowly twisted the knob and said in a way that made me feel really stupid, "You left your dome light on." His eyes scowled in a what-kind-of-an-idiot-are-you sort of way. Sure enough, I remembered twisting the knob last night to look for a pen that had dropped out of my bag. Apparently I forgot to twist it back.

He then ordered me to get the battery charger out of the shed. That's the other thing I'm pretty good at. Besides being an excellent light holder, I make a pretty good go-fer. Due to my inability to work with all things mechanical, I'm basically a handy man's nurse.

We put the battery charger on and proceeded to go back in the house. I went to the basement to play some guitar, and he went back to his recliner to watch TV. After a few hours, we went back out and the *old girl* fired right up. "Thanks, Dad," I managed to say over the humming motor.

And just like any man of few words, he said, "Sure."

Instead of going back in the house to lounge around, I decided to go for a quick bite at Gretchen's. Sitting at the bar with my plate of steak fries and an ice cold Coke allowed me to forget about teaching for a while. Sitting by myself with no one to talk to can be somewhat relaxing, though I would much rather have had a trusted friend to share the time with. *Sure would be nice to meet a fine girl,* I thought to myself. Thinking back to my girlfriend from college, I wondered what she was up to, and the thought of giving her a call entered my mind. Though the break-up was fairly amicable, she had refused my last-ditch effort to keep it going, which left me feeling even worse. I knew better than to give her a call. Not only was I was too proud to go crawling back, I didn't need to hear about her latest boyfriend. But when you're desperate for relationships, it's amazing how far you're willing to go sometimes.

My daydreaming about days gone by was interrupted suddenly by a blur passing outside the window in front of Gretchen's. About two seconds later, the blur walked inside. It was a young woman, approximately the same age as I am. Very good-looking, in my opinion, though she seemed uncomfortable. Almost as if she were scanning the room looking for a blind date. *Please, please, please, don't be here for a date.* I stared for roughly four seconds, until our eyes met, at which point I immediately looked down at my fries. "Sit anywhere you like, sweetie," came Gretchen's voice from behind the bar. I was hoping she'd sit close enough that I could look at her without being too obvious. Insecure guys like myself love to be in a position to look at lovely women. We just don't want to be spotted doing it.

Sure enough, she sat down in the exact spot I had picked out for her in my mind. She sat down a few tables away, facing the bar, allowing me to have a great view of the right side of her head. She was wearing blue jeans, a sweatshirt, and a baseball cap. My kind of girl. In only a few seconds of observation, I gathered she was probably very down-to-earth. Her left hand was out of view, making it hard to tell if she was married. Unfortunately, she was sitting just out of range for my ears to hear what she was saying to Gretchen. Besides taking her food order, it was clear there was more to the conversation. Things got very awkward when Gretchen turned in my direction and pointed. Then she laughed. My eyes went right back to my fries, so who knows what happened after that.

I was tempted to buy more food so I could hang out longer and see what this mystery woman was all about, but being low on cash solved that problem. I had lofty thoughts of asking her out, but I knew better. Guys like me don't walk up to strange women and ask them out on dates. Some of my friends in college occasionally told comparable stories, but I never actually saw them do it, leaving me to believe it probably only happens in movies.

I wish I had the courage to buy her a drink or leave a cute note on a napkin. Usually in the movies, the girl is the one who leaves a cute note with something like *Call Me!* along with a phone number. If only it could be that easy.

In high school, it was not uncommon for me to fall in love with several women at once. I had learned the most important rule about having a crush on someone in the second grade. DON'T TELL ANYONE! I once made the mistake of telling Clip about a girl I liked. Never again. He promised he wouldn't tell. We even pinky-swore on his mother's grave, though she wasn't dead, so perhaps that would explain why he blabbed. By the end of the day, everyone in class knew who I liked, which wouldn't have been bad except the look on her face made it clear she found me utterly disgusting. Every time she looked at me for the next month, her face got all contorted like she was eating lemons. I felt like crying, but I knew better. The kids in my class didn't need any additional ammunition to make my life more difficult.

One of the best things about having a secret crush on someone is playing around with the hope that things might actually work out. Even if the other person already has a boyfriend, there was always the chance, deep down, she really wanted to be with me. Maybe she was just dating the other person to pass the time until I asked her out. I knew better. There was a better chance of our basketball team winning a state title. (The same basketball team with the state record for most consecutive losses.)

The bathrooms in our high school were perfect for stalkers like me. Not creepy stalkers, just the I'm-a-bit-shy-and-would-rather-not-be-spotted kind of stalkers. If I stood in just the right place, the mirror by the sink allowed me to look out in the hallway and watch kids walk by. Clip and I had tested this out one day during study hall. I would go in the bathroom, stand by the sink, and wait for him to walk by. Every time he walked past, I could see him clearly, but he admitted a short while later that he couldn't see me. Then we'd switch it up. I imagined this is how a sniper must feel.

So, almost every day for four years, I'd wait after the last class in the bathroom for my dream girl to walk past. Once she passed, I'd walk out and follow her out of the school. Again, not close enough to get caught, but close enough that I could see what kind of jeans she was wearing. It was great. Never once did I get busted. There were some close calls, but I always put my head down and looked the other way.

The great thing about liking more than one girl was that there was always someone to fall back on. More than once I'd seen my number one prospect talking intensely or holding hands with her boyfriend. No problem. After a few minutes of rationalizing things in my head, the girl in my number two spot would just move up to the newly vacated top spot.

As is always the case, I left Gretchen's without doing anything risky. Sure, it would eat me up for a day or two, wishing I'd done something dicey (like ask this girl out), but I had enough going on with school that it would soon be forgotten.

Waking up the next morning and realizing that it actually was Friday helped get me moving. There's just something about that Friday-feel. Even the toughest situations seem a little less heavy on a Friday. Knowing I only had to get through a few more hours with my class before the weekend made the day palatable. The issues and problems I was facing in class were happening so frequently that they just sort of blended together.

Sitting down at my desk at the end of the day on Friday left me feeling hollow and discouraged. I didn't want to be here anymore. My stomach felt like it was loaded down with gravel that wanted to come up. That's when I looked up from my desk and saw it. A piece of folded notebook paper lying on the floor at the back of the room. Rising up out of my seat, I slowly walked over to pick it up. Slowly I unfolded it. My heart sank as I read its contents. Two girls had shared their thoughts the old-fashioned way…a note.

Are you as board as I am?

More.

I hate this class. Mr. Carter is soooo boring.

Yea, I know. He's prolly worse than Mr. Hairball.

No kidding! I think he hates us. All he does is yell at us and tell us how dum we are all the time.

I know. I wish we could get out of here. Get back to work! I think he saw us!

The sting felt by those words lingered long into the weekend. Taking a few hours to visit my grandma on Saturday evening was enough to numb the pain for a while. Since my grandpa died, my grandma had continued to live alone, never remarrying. She was my *fun* grandma. Her sunny disposition and positive outlook made it easy to stop by for an occasional visit. She loved to play board games and showed no mercy in beating me at checkers three times in a row.

"How about we do some baking?" I suggested after getting trounced for the third time. "Let's make chocolate chip cookies."

"Get the flour, sugar, and chocolate chips out of the pantry," she ordered. "I'll get everything else." For the next hour and a half, we baked cookies and drank milk while working on a crossword together. It might seem strange to see a guy spend a Saturday night with his grandma, but to me, it was time well spent. I knew she wasn't going to live forever, and I needed to take advantage of these particular opportunities.

It was back to the same old routine on Monday morning. Park the car, deposit my lunch in the refrigerator in the staff lounge, head to my classroom. I knew my fuse was short when I opened the refrigerator door to put my lunch inside and saw there was absolutely no room due to the overabundance of stuff. I immediately shoved three containers full of some long-since spoiled food toward the back of the fridge. I pushed them so hard, one of the containers broke open, causing a purplish gelatinous substance to spill all over the shelf and down the back wall of the fridge.

What is it with these people around here? Why don't we see how much garbage we can collect in this thing, I thought sarcastically. Looking around to see if anyone was watching, I grabbed an armload of plastic containers and marched over to the trash and heaved them in. Scores of old, half-eaten lunches lay there pleading to be put out of their misery. When I was finally done throwing away spoiled milk, moldy sandwiches, and unidentifiable foods, there were three shelves just waiting for fresh provisions. "Good work," I said to myself. Deep down I knew I had thrown away some things people might need, but when you're feeling ornery, that's a risk you're willing to take.

"Are we going to do anything fun today?" was the first thing one of my students said to me this morning. No "Hello." No "Hey, Mr. C, what's up?" Nothing. About ten seconds later, another student said, "Can we *not* do reading or math today? They're so boring."

I was so mad I couldn't even think of a good comeback. At least one I could say in front of them. *Maybe if you put a little effort into your work, you wouldn't be so bored,* I thought of later. I've never been one to have a quick comeback. It's only after the conversation has moved on to another topic, or sometimes days or weeks later, that I think of something clever. If time travel were possible, most of my trips would be used to go back and deliver verbal knockouts to anyone who had offended me.

Sure enough, my housekeeping was a hot topic during lunch. "Did you throw a bunch of stuff out of the fridge this morning?" Fran Helman asked me point-blank when I walked in the lounge to sit down. Her body language had *peeved* written all over it.

To avoid a flat-out lie, I returned her question with a question of my own. "What happened?" I asked, trying to sound as in-the-dark as possible.

"Somebody threw away my Jell-O," she grumbled. "I was saving that for today. I made it with my granddaughter last Thursday. It was grape Jell-O. My favorite."

"Some of my stuff got thrown away too," Julie Denkins whined. "I don't know who put themselves in charge around here, but it would have been nice if they had checked with us first."

Gus Harble, who's always got something to add, came through for once when he said, "I'm glad somebody cleaned that thing out. When something is no longer identifiable, it should be thrown away."

"Well, all I'm saying," Julie said huffily, "is whoever threw our stuff out should have asked first."

With any luck, Frank was probably the prime suspect, and he didn't care what anyone thought. He'd probably get a kick out of being blamed.

Later that afternoon, we attempted mathematics. Another disaster. After confusing most of the class, and myself as well, on the order of operations involved in adding fractions, we plodded through the rest of the lesson. Thank goodness for teacher's editions. Working my way through some of these problems reminded me of the time I was twelve and going through a haunted house. A lot of uncertainty with every move. My stomach churned through most of the problems. On more than one occasion, I just stopped and gave them the answer provided by the teacher's manual because I had not only baffled them, I was a bit bewildered myself.

"I'm confused," more than one student said.

"Well, are you listening?" came my response. "If you listened, you wouldn't be so confused."

"Yeah, but...you seem a little confused too," said Steven Dooley, who never had a problem expressing his opinion.

These kids could be so annoying. "Do I?" I said in a haughty manner. "Try paying attention for once. See what happens. See if the number of times you ask dumb questions decreases."

I didn't know where this was going, and then I did something really stupid. It's too bad I didn't realize the stupidity of my ways until it was too late. Walking over to the board, I drew the outline for a graph. Because this episode was unscripted, my graph made little to no sense. "Let's put a dot right here. Here's where you are when you don't pay attention." Removing the top from my marker, I made a black dot way up on the left side of the graph. "Now, we'll keep track of your dumb questions over a five-day period. Remember class, we're trying to see if there's a correlation between not paying attention and asking stupid questions."

Looking at his face, it was hard to tell if he was more embarrassed or just plain ticked off. *Good,* I thought. Chalk one up for the teacher. This class was going to give me the respect I deserved one way or another. Yes, I would have preferred that they just give it to me, but if they were choosing not to, it was up to me to pull it out of them.

Nothing shuts up a class like a long, tedious assignment. The only time this class was quiet for more than three minutes was after a heavy load of reading from a textbook and answering a series of questions at the end of the lesson. Sitting on my stool, I felt more like an owl sitting on a branch watching for the slightest movement than a classroom teacher. Watching and waiting to attack anyone who stepped out of line. The animosity between myself and my class was a living, growing entity about to explode within the confines of my soul.

Silence filled the room. Not a good one, either. It was the

kind of stillness I imagined existing on battle fields during the Revolutionary War, with both sides facing each other, ready to put an end to each other's existence, shortly before the cannons and muskets fired. If these kids wanted a war, they were going to get one.

As I was trying to get answers out of some of these kids, I noticed a pattern. There are certain kids who never seem to have the right answer. And it is those same students who always have their hand in the air. Wouldn't it be great if somebody could invent a device that would prevent these kids from raising their hand? Just the pleasure in knowing some child who thrives on giving stupid answers and always wants to raise his hand, but can't, would be satisfaction enough. Now that I think of it, duct tape would be a lot more practical.

In the afternoon, we made an effort at English. "Boys and girls," I said, "every sentence must contain two things. Raise your hand if you know what those two things are."

One of my attention-seeking students raised his hand. "Um...I think it's a denominator and a noun, right?" *Go tear off a piece of duct tape.*

November means Parent-Teacher Conferences. With all the training they give you in college, there's no class on how to conduct PTC's. As a kid, I always wondered what my teachers were saying to my parents. My brother and I would be at home on pins and needles waiting for our mom and dad to return. I figured my teachers must have focused on the negative more than the positive because the first thing my dad would say was, "What's going on with you and Clip? Your teacher said she had to move you two because you were talking too much." *Well, yeah, but did she mention I had raised my hand twice yesterday and gave her CORRECT answers? Did she say anything about all my work being done on time? Had she mentioned the fact that I found Julie White's green eraser on the floor and RETURNED it to her?* Apparently not.

My hands were so sweaty; I kept a wad of tissues in both front pockets of my pants to mop up the perspiration that was oozing from my palms. A few of the parents wiped their hands on their pants or coat right after shaking my hand. Their actions, unbeknownst to them, were whittling away what little confidence I had left. As the night wore on, I found myself saying the same things over and over. *Your son needs to pay attention more. He's doing a lot of talking when he's supposed to be listening. Your child needs to stop blurting out so much.* I felt like a broken record. Too bad my class was full of boneheads.

When Bryan Brookens' mom entered my room at 7:30 p.m. on Thursday night, I I'd never seen a woman who looked so beaten down or so tired. The look on her face showed that she knew exactly what was coming—fifteen minutes of me talking about how awful her son had been for the past two-and-half months, how he needs to straighten up and fly right if he wants to see the seventh grade. I was ready for her, feeling like a lawyer ready to convict her child of being the meanest, rudest waste of skin there ever was. I didn't want to start off too strong, so I stuck out my hand and introduced myself. "Hi, Mrs. Brookens," I said. "Thanks for coming tonight." I don't recall her giving any sort of opening for a response. "How's everything going?"

"Let's just cut to the chase here, Mr. Carter," she said. "I know you don't like Bryan, and to be perfectly honest, he's not really fond of you either." I felt like I'd just been sucker punched in the gut. "He hates school, and quite honestly, I don't know what I'm going to do with him," she continued. "Since his father passed away, he's been nothing but trouble. I work until 6:00 almost every night, so I'm not around to make sure he's gettin' done the things that need gettin' done."

"I'm sorry to hear about your husband," I interjected.

"Oh, he wasn't my husband." Then came a very awkward silence.

"Oh," was all I could manage.

"I adopted Bryan when he was eight years old," she told me. "He's had a very difficult life in his twelve short years. When he was three months old, his momma went off and left him and his daddy by themselves. His father made some poor choices that led Bryan into foster care. I won't go into all the details, Mr. Carter, but he's been in situations you can't imagine and had things done to him that no child should ever have to endure...by people he should've been able to trust." She waited a second before continuing. "I adopted him three years ago. He used to visit his father twice a month in Detroit, until he died last year in a house fire. I think it had something to do with drugs; we're not real sure. But anyway, Bryan's been really hard to live with this past year."

"I understand," I said, trying to sound like I really *did* understand.

"No, Mr. Carter, I don't think you do understand," she said, sounding a little bit annoyed. "You have no idea what this boy's been through. If you did, you might try to be more aware as to who's sitting in these chairs every day."

Talk about feeling like a complete and total idiot. I don't even remember what I told her from that point on, and I'm sure she wasn't really listening anyway. Feeling about two inches tall, I walked her to the door and told her to have a nice evening, though I'm almost certain she was done listening to what I had to say a long time ago.

Wandering back to my desk, I stopped at Bryan's seat and sat down. Perhaps I was trying to get a better understanding of what it felt like to be in his shoes, but of course I couldn't really do that. I felt terrible. It finally hit me. I wasn't cut out for teaching. Realizing that I'd made the biggest mistake in my life, I began to plan my resignation.

I imagine it would be difficult with any job knowing you're planning to quit, but showing up anyway and going through the motions had a way of sucking away what little life was left in me. I was faking it. My only emotion...numbness. I no longer cared what happened. During the next few days, the class didn't seem as rowdy, but it didn't matter. It was more than likely because I didn't care anymore. My mind was made up. I just had to wait for my opportunity to tell Boggins I was done. He'd probably scowl at me and tell me how disappointed he was, but I didn't care, because it didn't matter; I was done. Nothing mattered anymore. The past four years had been a total waste of time. My teaching degree was a total bust. I'd probably end up at the lumber yard again, trying to make ends meet and, of course, still living with my parents.

The worst part of this whole mess was that I felt completely and totally alone. I felt like the only guy in the world who might feel this way. Alone. Deserted. Inside…I was dead. What was once a living, vibrant heart was now stone cold and completely lifeless. I'm assuming this is what depression feels like. I wasn't going to do anything drastic, like take a bunch of pills or blow my head off with a shotgun, but I won't say those thoughts hadn't entered my mind. If I were to put an end to it all, I wondered who would come to my funeral. Would people even miss me? Maybe all the girls I had dated in the past would show up crying their eyes out because I was gone; their small embers of hope that maybe, just maybe, things would've worked out if we'd just tried a little harder would have been snuffed out. Doubt it. My parents would probably be a little ticked, not because I was gone, but because the extra money they got from me for room and board would be gone too.

Walking to the office on Friday afternoon to resign seemed strange. I'd walked these halls so many times as a kid. Wouldn't it be cool to be that kid again? Life seemed so easy back then. My biggest worry had been whether anyone would notice that I only had two pairs of pants, which I wore on an alternating basis. One week it'd be Monday, Wednesday, Friday for one pair, and the next week they'd be my Tuesday, Thursday pants. I'd love for that to be my biggest concern again.

I walked into the office like a bad dog who'd let down his master. With tail tucked between my legs, I shuffled past the secretary on my way to see Boggins. "He left for the weekend, Ted," said Carol, as I looked through the door window to his darkened office. "Do you need something?" she asked.

"No," I lied. "I just wanted to see if he was around. No big deal. I'll see him on Monday." *Oh no,* I thought, *now I have to come back.* "Can I get his home number in case I need to get a hold of him this weekend?" I asked.

"Sure," she replied. She took a pink sticky note and quickly scribbled the seven digits that made up his phone number. "Here you go. Are you sure it's nothing important?" she asked, obviously realizing that something was on my mind.

"Yeah, it's no big deal," I told her. "I'd just hate to have to get in touch with him and not have his number."

"Okay," she said, "but I think I overheard him say something about heading up to his cottage, so I'll give you that number too."

"Thanks, Carol," I said. "Have a good weekend," I told her with about as much enthusiasm as a sloth.

"You too, Ted. See you next week."

Talk about frustrating; I couldn't even quit.

"I need something cold," I told Gretchen, moping my way up to the bar.

"It looks like you need more than that," came her reply. "I've seen corpses with more life in them than you've got. What's your problem?"

"I think I made a huge mistake."

"Oh yeah, what's that?"

"I'm getting a sneaking suspicion that teaching is not for me."

"What makes you say that?" she asked.

"Oh, just the fact that I can't stand the kids in my class, and I hate trying to teach them stuff when all they want to do is goof off."

"Lighten up," she said, "that's what kids do."

"I don't know, Gretchen. I'm tired of being treated like a second class citizen by a bunch of mangy, spoiled brats."

"What in the name of everything splendid do you think you were like when you were that age? You know what?" she continued, "Don't answer that. I'll tell you. You were just like those sorry bums sitting in front of you all day."

"Get outta here," I responded. "If I acted half as dopey as these kids, my ol' man would've let me have it."

"News flash," she said, "You weren't half as perfect as you think you were."

"Yeah, but at least I grew out of it. I certainly don't act like that anymore."

"Okay," she replied. "You're also twice their age."

Good point, I thought to myself.

"So don't go acting all holier-than-thou, Teddy. If you expect these kids to walk into your room, sit down, and wait for you to pour your knowledge into them, you've got another thing coming, mister. This is what kids do. You didn't make it easy for your teachers, and now it's coming right back in your face. The truth of the matter is that you're scared. You think you gotta tell 'em what to do all the time or else you'll lose control of 'em. Well...how's that working for ya?"

I didn't even bother to respond. I'd been around Gretchen enough to know that she knew what she was saying. Tipping my glass back and looking towards the bottom, I secretly wished there was a switch I could flip to make this class different. Then a crazy thought entered my brain. Maybe I could tell the police someone was threatening me, and the only way for me to move on with my life would be to participate in the Witness Protection Program. With the help of the federal government, I could search for a utopian society to quietly graft into. I knew getting a job here was a big mistake.

CHAPTER 8

A Chance Encounter

What in the world was I supposed to do now? The year wasn't even half over, and I had no idea what I was going to do next. After mulling it over during the weekend, I decided against an immediate resignation. It was early December, and the promise of getting two weeks away from this class provided just enough motivation to wake up and get through the day. Maybe the best thing to do would be to tell Boggins on the last day before Christmas vacation, giving him two weeks to find a replacement.

About three days before the holiday break, I managed to get so mad at one point that I had to walk out into the hallway because I didn't want to hurt anyone. What little patience was left inside had evaporated. Being in the middle of a horrible cold made every inconvenience and annoying situation even worse. I was incredibly crabby, and things were not going well.

Trying to teach was impossible. There were about a hundred things more interesting than me. They were constantly looking around the room and out the window, focused on everything but me.

The tension in the room finally reached the breaking point. It all started with one teeny, tiny snowflake. I don't even remember who spotted it first, but the next thing I knew, there were about fifteen kids over by the window trying to look out at the itty-bitty, microscopic flakes of snow. "Excuse me," I said, "I'm trying to teach here. Everybody sit down." Then I raised my voice and screamed, "NOW!" Taking their sweet time and mumbling to themselves, they ambled back to their seats while I went over and closed the blinds. "This is Michigan…it snows here. Get used to it!" I yelled.

In a rare moment of charity, I let them watch a movie on the last day before vacation. We had to stop it about twelve times because they were talking so loud. I wasn't too surprised. Try and do something nice, and they can't even be thankful enough to keep their mouths shut. Bryan and Steven kept finishing the lines before the actors. Several girls were writing notes. Two kids were sleeping, while several others felt it their duty to shush the ones who were talking. "If you guys can't be quiet, I'll turn this thing off," I threatened several times, secretly hoping they'd shut up, because I really had nothing else for them to do. They didn't feel like learning, and I definitely didn't feel like teaching. "If you can't shut up, we'll get the math books out." *That'll teach 'em,* I thought. It took us over two hours to watch a ninety minute movie with all the interruptions and distractions.

Finally, at the end of the day, I half-heartedly wished them a Merry Christmas as they practically ran out of the room. "Yee haw!" they screamed. "No more school!" which I interpreted as, *No Mr. Carter for two weeks!*

It was very difficult having to walk by Kim Busche's room and see her desk piled with presents from all her adoring students, causing me to despise her even more. Judging by the amount of stuff she had, it would take at least three trips to her car. There were gift boxes and bags all over the place. Two days earlier, she was bragging about how much stuff her class from last year had given her: gift certificates to restaurants and book stores, along with all kinds of other treats and trinkets. And because they *just knew* she loved chocolate, there were more candy bars, Hershey kisses, and M&M's than she knew what to do with. Listening to her ramble on and on, it was clear she held herself in pretty high regard. Just as I walked past her door empty-handed, she was coming out with an armload of presents. *All right, it looks like she'll be making four trips out to her car.* "So what did your kids get you this year?" she asked. "What was your best present?" I knew she was going to ask that question. I was ready for it.

"Got a hundred dollar gift card to Rusty's Roadhouse," I muttered.

"Wow!" she said, feigning interest. "Not bad."

"Yup, should be able to get a couple of meals outta that one." Truth be told, I did get a gift card for Rusty's Roadhouse, but it was only for ten dollars. So I was off a little bit with the decimal point. Big deal. I didn't even bother asking what she got, because I didn't really care.

Watching her struggle with her load, I couldn't help thinking of how a real gentleman would help her carry things out to her car. Looking around, I didn't see one, so I quickened my pace, creating a sizable distance between us. *I hope she drops it all. It would serve her right.* I took great delight in letting the door slam shut as I walked out into the parking lot, forcing her to set some of her things down to push on the door handle.

Before I got into my car to go home, I remembered that I was going to tell Boggins I was resigning. The thought of going back in there and talking to him was a bit scary. I chickened out and drove home, eager to start my vacation.

Though I had no plans to do anything grandiose over vacation, I was looking forward to a break from that place. Two weeks with nothing but time on my hands. I was quite certain, though, that my parents would do their best to drive me nuts. But at this point, it seemed better than going to school.

The first few days were great. I didn't accomplish one solitary thing, unless you consider sitting on the couch in gray sweatpants a monumental achievement. Getting two weeks off during the holidays was the equivalent of that feeling you get when you finally work that irritating piece of popcorn from between your molars…times a hundred. Sleeping in, taking catnaps, and using the bathroom at the faintest inclination are just a few of the benefits of having time away from school. Looking at my face in the bathroom mirror one afternoon before Christmas, the dark, puffy circles under my eyes indicated a reprieve had been earned.

Like many of my experiences at school, what I hoped would happen over vacation didn't exactly pan out. My mother, who was trying to avoid gaining fifteen pounds over the holidays, had started a new morning routine of making some kind of breakfast shake involving the blender. At 6:00 in the morning! Why she couldn't wait to make it after I was up and around, I'll never know. Waking up to an alarm is one thing, but with the racket she was making out in the kitchen, she might just as well set up her little contraption at the side of my bed and push *liquefy*.

One thing I did accomplish was moving my bed all the way across the room, away from the wall next to the bathroom. My head had been about eight inches from the back of the toilet, and despite drywall and insulation, I could still hear some rather unpleasant sounds from the bathroom. I don't know which one of my parents was responsible, but every morning around 5:30 a.m. someone was in there banging around, and with my head only inches away from a gallon and a half of rushing water, there was no sleeping through it.

A few days before my brother and his wife were to come over for Christmas dinner, I volunteered to do some shopping for my mother. Anything to get out of the house. I was so desperate for dialogue with someone besides my parents, I didn't really care what form it took. Having someone ask me if I had coupons or bottle slips or if I wanted paper or plastic was something. My mother and I were starting to irritate each other just a bit too much. A guy can only take so much lying around in sweatpants and watching TV. Every time I went into the kitchen and opened the refrigerator door, she asked me what I wanted. "What are you looking for in there?" she'd wonder out loud.

"Nothing, mom. Seriously, can't a guy open the refrigerator door without feeling like he's been questioned by a German Gestapo?" I muttered under my breath.

After she handed me the grocery list, I scanned through it quickly. "Do I really need to buy your feminine products?" I asked in an agitated tone upon seeing a certain word written in cursive towards the bottom.

"It doesn't make sense for me to drive into town later for one thing, does it?"

"C'mon, Mom!" I pleaded, though I knew it wouldn't do any good. I didn't need to hear her go on and on about the things she does for me, so I just left.

It was while I was in college that I discovered the benefits of grocery shopping. Wandering the aisles and listening to elevator music can be very soothing. Leisurely browsing the rows has a way of settling the nerves. It's not quite the same as a back rub, but it's a close second.

Walking with my arms leaning on the crossbar of the cart, lifting my head occasionally to make sure I was on the right side, I made my way through the store. My heart began to beat a little faster with the thought of one my students being here too. We'd probably both look the other way.

I figured my best bet was to get the item my mother requested first and then fill in the other items around it. I slowly made my way to the aisle where the personal products were shelved. I felt a bit squeamish about what I had to do. My hand shook as I reached out and grabbed a box from the shelf and tossed it into the empty cart. Beads of sweat began to percolate on my forehead. Then I heard a familiar sound; the voice of Glen telling a customer the difference between his hamburger, which was ground right there in the store, and some of the leading brands. "You just don't know what you're getting with some of those other guys," he said. "I've heard some of those people put sawdust in their hamburger. Anything to make an extra buck," he went on. His voice faded as I snaked my way up and down the walkways. No doubt he was explaining how he uses only the best cuts of meat with no fillers. When I was six, I remember standing with my mother listening to the same spiel. Everyone in town knew the difference. Glen was a good guy. A bit talkative, but a good guy, nonetheless.

"Is that Ted Carter?" I heard a man's voice say behind me. *Son of a gun. I can't go anywhere without being bothered*, I thought. Obstinately, I refused to look behind me and kept going in a forward shuffle. Maybe I just imagined it.

"Ted, is that you?" *Okay, I wasn't imagining it.* Immediately, I reached for the first thing I could get my hands on. To hide the contents of the cart, I threw four loaves of rye bread on top of the box in an effort to avoid looking like some kind of weirdo. Deciding it would be in my best interest to turn around, I slowly glanced back over my shoulder. Standing ten yards away, down towards the end of the aisle, was my favorite teacher of all time: Mr. Fritz.

"Mr. Fritz!?!?" I said in question-like excitement. "How are you?"

"I'm doing just fine," he said, walking towards me. "How are you doing?"

"Not too bad," I said, even though inside I was feeling unhappy, lonely, and downright miserable. I was two steps from full-fledged depression, but when you run into someone you haven't seen in a number of years, let alone someone you look up to, you tend to fudge a little bit.

"How's school going?" he asked. "I heard you were teaching here in town. Things going okay?"

"Yeah, not too bad." I said, continuing the fib. "We just started vacation, and I'm looking forward to having some down time."

"You gotta be careful who you say that to," he said with a grin. "Not everybody gets two weeks off like teachers. Between you and me, though, I know you've earned it."

"I'll say," I said rather quickly.

"You know what," he said, "if you have time between the holidays, give me a call. I'd love to get together. It will be fun to see how one of my favorite students is handling himself as a teacher."

"That would be great."

"The missus and I will be out of town for a couple of days later this week, but feel free to give me a jingle if you're not doing anything." He paused for a moment. "I'll let you get back to your shopping." As he said the last sentence, we both looked at the contents of my cart. "Those are for your mom, right?" he said with a huge smile on his face. "Let me give you some advice. Get those things last; then you can tuck 'em under something else. Or better yet," he went on laughing, "buy a dishtowel to drape over that stuff."

Watching him walk away, I felt better for some reason. It was like he offered some sort of invisible peace, and just being in his presence was enough to catch a trace of it. Maybe it was because he called me one of his favorite students. It felt good to see him, and as I continued my shopping, I gave some serious consideration toward taking him up on his offer to get together.

Nothing ruins Christmas like getting older. When I was younger, my brother and I would wake up long before my parents, race down the hallway to the living room, and tear through our stockings like crazed animals. Now that I was older and my brother was out of the house, things were very different. I felt little else on Christmas morning except for a little gratitude that I didn't have to go to school.

Lying in bed in the early morning, my mind drifted to a handful of my students. Some of them were more than likely racing their brothers or sisters down the hallway to tear through their stockings. There were some, too, who probably didn't have much at all to look forward to this morning. Many of the kids in my class came from some unique situations, to say the least. Bryan was waking up this morning in a house full of people he wasn't even related to. A lot of other kids would be "hopping" from one house to another because their parents were divorced or separated. I figured some of those kids could easily end up being at four or five different houses throughout the day.

I also thought about quitting. If I was going to do it, this would be the time. After Christmas Day, of course. I figured I'd let Boggins enjoy the day with his family, but I knew I would have to make the call sooner or later.

"It'll be fun to see how one of my favorite students is handling himself as a teacher," I heard Mr. Fritz's voice say. *"If you have time, give me a call."* I laid there a bit longer, thinking about Christmas, teaching, how nice it would be to wake up with a family of my own someday on Christmas morning. Maybe things would be different if I had a wife and a couple of kids gathered around the tree.

I sat through Christmas dinner with a gaping hole in my soul. I feigned enthusiasm as my brother and sister-in-law announced they were pregnant and expecting a baby in early July. "How'd that happen?" my dad asked, to which he proceeded to be the only one laughing. This was his *expected* question, the one he asked everybody after that sort of announcement. After dinner we exchanged gift certificates, turned on the TV, and worked off our dinner by dozing in and out of consciousness.

As a kid, I loved the Christmas season. Christmas Eve had always been my favorite. Christmas Day could sometimes be a little anti-climatic, especially today as I wallowed in my loneliness. *I hope the rest of my life isn't like this,* I thought to myself.

Thank goodness for football. The Dallas Cowboys and Arizona Cardinals were engaged in a serious game on TV. A game that would decide whether or not the Cowboys would be in the playoffs. Though it periodically took my mind away from my own tribulations, I could barely concentrate on the game. My mind kept drifting back to Mr. Fritz. By the end of the third quarter, with the Cardinals up by fourteen, it looked like Dallas' season would be done in early January. They reminded me of myself. I could very easily be done in early January too. At least they would have something to look forward to next fall with a new season. I, on the other hand, had very little to look forward to. Depression has a way of swallowing you up in one big gulp, rolling you around in its mouth for a while, marinating you, and letting despair permeate your entire being. I had two choices. I could call Boggins tomorrow and quit, or I could call Mr. Fritz to set up a time to get together. After the game, I summoned what little life was left in my body and went to bed. I ended the day in much the same way as it began. Alone in bed. Confused. Uncertain of what to do next. My brain said, "Quit," while my heart said, "Let's just wait and see what Mr. Fritz has to say."

Driving to Tim Fritz's house was a little bit nerve-wracking. I had nothing to be afraid of, yet for some reason my stomach was doing flip-flops. I had called him last night to see if I could drop by for a visit. I couldn't help but wonder what he did that made me not only like his class so much, but him as well.

It was another bright morning. Cold. But at least the sun was shining. I got out of my car and walked up the steps to his brick ranch on the east end of town. Approaching the door, I could see him sitting at his kitchen table, cup of coffee in one hand and a section of the newspaper in the other. *What a life,* I thought. *Every day is like a Saturday for this guy.*

I knocked lightly on the door and waited a few seconds. "Come on in," his wife said, opening the door after I rang the doorbell. "Tim's been waiting for you." I stepped inside, and she closed the door behind me. "Here, let me have your coat," she said, helping me take it off. "And don't worry about your shoes. Our house isn't so nice that people can't walk through here with their shoes on. You haven't stepped in anything, have you?" she asked with a grin.

I could only smile. "Thanks, Mrs. Fritz," I said. "I'm glad he could take some time to see me." Here I was again, not knowing what to call someone. Calling him Tim seemed almost disrespectful.

"Hey, Ted, have a seat." He stood up from the kitchen table and gave me his signature two-handed handshake. The kind where you take your non-shaking hand and place it over the other person's hand. "Man, am I glad to see you. I hope you don't think it was weird for me to invite you over. I'm sure you have better things to do than hang around with some old guy."

"Well, I had a few breaks in my schedule," I said with a grin. Who was I kidding? I had nothing planned for two whole weeks except for the Christmas dinner I'd already had with my family. So far, the highlight of my entire vacation had been watching *A Christmas Story* by myself while my dad slept in his recliner and my mom slept on the couch.

"It was so cool seeing you at Glen's last week," he said. "It's kind of fun to see former students once in a while."

"That's because kids liked you," I said, catching myself by surprise. I didn't really mean to say that, even though it was true. "You know," I continued, "kids kind of liked being in your class. You were a fun teacher."

"Thanks, Ted," he said. "Can I get you a cup of coffee?" he asked.

"Sure, that'd be great."

"By the way, in case you're wondering, call me Tim. You're over the legal limit, so let's keep it on the lighter side." Pouring me a cup, he asked, "Cream or sugar?"

"Both," I replied.

He came over with my cup of coffee in one hand and cream and sugar in the other. Walking back to get me a spoon, he said, "I couldn't help but think back on our conversation the other day. I know you said things were going okay. I believe your exact words were '*not too bad.*' The grocery store isn't always the best place to hold a conversation, so that's why I invited you to stop by. I thought maybe it would be good for you to have someone to talk teaching with. I thought maybe we could have a real conversation about how things were going." He stopped for a second then went on. "I remember my first few years of teaching. It's a wonder I stuck with it at all. You know, I almost quit halfway through my first year."

Hearing him say that was like slowly letting the air out of balloon, except instead of air, it was anxiety and tension that seemed to ease out of my pores.

"I had just about had it with that particular class of wing nuts. To this day, that was one of the toughest groups ever assembled. Something about the chemistry in that class." He stopped for a moment. "Teaching can be pretty tough at times, and I just wanted to see how thing were *really* going for you. Before you answer that, let's go sit in the living room."

Wow, this isn't what I was expecting, I thought to myself.

"So how is it going?" he asked. "How's it *really* going?"

"Well," I said slowly, not really sure how to even begin, "I think I might have made a huge mistake going into teaching. Though listening to what you just said kind of makes me feel a little better, knowing that you struggled too."

He just sat there for a minute. "You know what?" he asked. Without waiting for me to reply he continued, "You are not alone, Ted. I don't know what it is about us, but it's so hard sometimes to openly admit when we're struggling. Sure, we feel it on the inside, but to tell somebody about it can be tough. It's like we can't own up to the fact that there are times when life just sucks. It's like we think it's a weakness to tell somebody else we're struggling." I laughed when he said *sucks* because I distinctly remember him telling Clip to never use that word in his class again.

He was right. There was nobody in my life with whom I could be totally honest. Nobody to whom I could just say, "Hey, I'm having a hard time, and I don't know what to do." Deep down, I wanted everyone to think that I had it all together.

"To be perfectly honest, I hate teaching," I said.

He looked right at me and said, "You know what? It takes a lot of guts to admit that. So you hate teaching; now what are going to do? Are you going to stop right now...in the middle of the year?"

"I have no idea," I mumbled. "Every morning I wake up with a knot in my stomach. My appetite is gone. Teaching is nothing like I thought it was going to be. I guess I never really knew what to expect. I thought I'd walk into the classroom, and kids would love seeing me. I thought they might want to learn something. But right now, I can't stand getting out of bed in the morning, knowing I have to face those kids. I hate it."

"I know this isn't going to solve your problem," he said, "but I can relate to how you feel. Like I said, I wanted nothing more than to throw it all away during my first year too."

I interrupted. "It's hard to imagine that you wanted to quit teaching. Everybody loved you."

"Let me ask you something, Ted," he said, leaning forward. "What did I teach you?'

"Math," I said.

"No, I mean, what specifically did I teach you?"

"Um...I don't know. I think you may have taught me how to add and subtract fractions." Looking down at the floor and waiting a moment to think, I added, "Seems like I remember hearing the word reciprocal in your class, but don't ask me to tell you what it means." When I looked up, he was smiling.

"Is that all?"

"I don't know; I can't really think of anything else. I remember sitting in your class, working, listening to you talk about things. Sometimes it was about math, and sometimes it wasn't."

"So you spent an entire year in my class, and that's all you can think of?" he asked with a look of chagrin.

"I'm sorry....I guess that's it," I said, feeling a little bit ashamed of myself. It did seem a little unusual that that was all I could re-member. After having a moment to reflect, I continued, "One of my fondest memories was sitting in your class after Rick Edwards got in that bad accident, and we all thought he was going to die. We just talked the whole class period."

"Sure, I remember that," he said, nodding his head. "I could tell by the way everybody was walking around that math was not going to be a priority that day."

"It seemed like all our other teachers wanted to go on with busi-ness as usual, like Rick's accident was no big deal. You, on the other hand, treated us like real human beings."

"I know," he said. "And that is what made all the difference. If all you ever learned from me was how to do math problems, then I wouldn't consider our time together very successful."

"What do you mean?"

"What I mean...is that there's more to *me* being a teacher than just helping my students get better at math."

"Yeah, but weren't you paid to teach us math?"

"Sure I was, but I realized early in my career that when I only talked about math, kids didn't like coming to my class, and that really bothered me."

Just then, he started to laugh. "What's so funny?" I asked.

"I was just thinking of a time during my first year when I got so upset I actually tipped a desk over."

Hearing him say that made me laugh too. "Was anyone sitting in it?" I asked dryly.

"No, thank goodness. And while it got their attention, it did nothing to improve the atmosphere in my classroom. If anything, it caused them to lose even more respect for me."

He continued, "I had to find a way to get them excited about being in my class even if they weren't excited about doing math. I realized after teaching a few years that kids didn't like me. I figured the reason they didn't like me was because they weren't any good at math. It made sense to me, but I didn't like how I felt inside. I kept telling myself it wasn't my fault these kids hated math, but I never really believed it. My defining moment came when I was walking downtown on a Saturday afternoon, doing some shopping, and I saw a few of my students on the other side of the street. I went in the first door I could find, because the thought of any kind of an encounter terrified me."

"So what did you do?" I asked.

"Sometimes we have to hit the floor before we can make an accurate assessment, and it finally dawned on me that I had pretty much made a wreckage of everything by doing things my way, and I knew things weren't going to get any better if I continued doing what I was doing."

When he stopped to sip his coffee, it gave my brain a chance to comprehend what he was telling me. Then he went on. "I realized shortly into my teaching career that doing dumb things is a lot like stepping in dog poop," he said. "You end up carrying it around for a while."

I wasn't sure exactly what he was getting at with his analogy. He went on, "When I yelled at kids, or did things to embarrass them, I caused a lot more damage than I realized."

"That sounds a lot like me," I told him. "I know the kids don't like me, and I guess I don't blame them."

He continued. "Sometimes as teachers we don't understand how our actions affect kids. Just because they don't look embarrassed or upset doesn't mean their feelings haven't been hurt." He paused again, almost as if he knew I needed to hear every word he was saying. "It took a long time for me to change my reputation. It was one of the hardest things I've ever had to do, but there are two things that have made all the difference."

"Are you going to let me in on the secret?" I wondered out loud.

He began by saying, "For starters, my faith has been a big factor. It's kind of hard to put into words, but what I can tell you is that I reached a point where I needed some answers. Answers to questions like 'Why am I here?' and 'What's my purpose?'"

Without hesitating he went on, "The other thing that's helped has been finding people I can be totally honest with about the joys and struggles this world has thrown my way. Having a relationship with someone I know really cares about me has given me the freedom to grow and ultimately helped answer some of those questions too."

Before he said any more, he took a quick sip of his coffee. "Trying to go through this world on your own will only lead to destruction."

Just like an invisible puzzle, his words slid right into the vacant areas of my heart. As they snapped into place, things started to make sense. He had just described the last few months of my life in one sentence.

The knot of anxiety in my gut that I felt towards school had begun to loosen a teeny-tiny bit. Unfortunately, it was so tight that I wasn't sure it would ever unravel.

"Suppose I were to ask one of your students, 'How does Mr. Carter treat you?' What do you think they'd say?"

"I don't want to know the answer to that," I said matter-of-factly.

"Do you yell at them?"

"Sometimes."

"Why?" he asked.

"Because…they don't listen to me."

"How's that working out for you?" he asked, sounding a lot like Gretchen.

"It works most of the time," I replied.

"Do you think that makes them want to be in your class?"

"Probably not."

He continued, "Do you ever remember me yelling at you or another person in class?"

"No."

"I'll be honest with you," he said. "Sometimes I do yell. Just the other night, I yelled at the TV when the Cowboys missed a field goal." He closed his eyes and laughed for a brief moment before continuing. "It's sad, but I used to yell at the kids in my class too, especially during my first few years. I could scream and holler with the best of 'em. I used to get into these little arguments all the time with kids. What I learned over time was that getting into a confrontation with a kid in class was a lot like getting into a fight with a skunk. By the time it was all over, we both stunk, and nobody won. But like I said, kids didn't like me, and they definitely didn't want to be in my classroom."

"So how did you change things?" I asked.

"Well, it didn't happen overnight, but I finally realized what these kids needed. You see, Ted, these kids don't care how smart you are or how much you know; the only things they're worried about is whether or not you care about them. You see, teaching, whether it happens in a classroom or not, won't be very effective if there isn't a healthy relationship."

Ouch. As I sat there, I felt this numbness slowly spread throughout my entire body. My arms and legs felt like they weighed a hundred pounds each. I knew that I didn't care about my kids.

His words sliced through the air, breaking the temporary silence, "Teaching has nothing to do with transferring information from one brain to another. It has everything to do with connecting your heart with the hearts of those kids in your class. It's only through their hearts that you'll be able to transform their minds.

"Let me ask you something else," he continued. "If I asked one of your students, 'Does Mr. Carter care about you?' what do you think they'd say?"

"I don't think I want to know the answer to that one either," I stammered, "but I'm pretty sure they'd say 'no.'"

"What I can tell you, Ted, is that I've been in your shoes before, so I know how uncomfortable it is. Let me ask you another question. Do you think I enjoyed teaching?"

"Yeah."

"You're right. I did enjoy teaching once I figured out it was more than shoving information at kids." He went quiet for a moment, then asked, "How can you tell if someone enjoys teaching?" he asked as if he didn't know the answer.

"Well," I stammered, "for starters….they'd probably have a smile on their face most of the time. Maybe they'd be excited about what they're teaching," I continued.

"Do you think I was more excited to teach math, or do you think I was more excited to get to know kids like you?"

"Uh….it seemed like you were more excited to see me."

"You're absolutely right," he said. "You see, I realized by the time you came along that kids didn't care how much I knew. Like I said a minute ago, kids don't care how much you know until they know how much you care. I know it sounds cliché, but it's true. When kids think you don't care about them, they aren't going to give a hoot about what you have to say. I don't want to brag, but you know what? Eventually, I reached a point where I could get kids to do what I asked. Not because I made them, mind you, but because we had the kind of relationship where we cared about each other, we respected each other, and we liked each other. When you're in that kind of relationship, people will do amazing things for each other. So in my case, if I asked the kids to do the odd *and* the even math problems, they did them."

"Yeah, I remember," I replied. "There were a couple of times when you gave us a little extra work because we were getting a little squirrely."

"Do you ever remember me yelling?" he asked.

"No, but I know there were times we let you down."

"Exactly," he said. "There are always going to be times in any relationship when people let each other down. Right, dear?" he said, winking at his wife who had just come through the living room carrying a laundry basket full of clothes.

"That's right," she said, smiling and returning his wink.

"I'm not sure if you remember Mrs. Feely?" he asked. "She taught at Coleman for..." Then he paused. "Quite a while."

"Yeah, I had her for eighth grade social studies," I said with a little chuckle.

"Why are you laughing?"

"Because we used get such a rush watching her explode all the time. It was a game to see how quickly we could get her up on her desk to scream and yell at us."

"I bet that was fun to watch," he said. "Now I'm not trying to put her down, but she had no business being in front of children for thirty years. Outside of school, she was and still is a very nice person, but she had no idea how to run a classroom."

"I'll say," I said without thinking about it.

"Well, guess what, Ted?" he said, lowering his head and raising an eyebrow at me, which was all he needed to say. I was on a fast track to becoming the next Ruth Feely. "You've got some things to think about so you don't end up like Ruth and become the laughingstock of the school. Change isn't going to come easy, and don't be surprised if you get some resistance at first. And don't expect these kids to change overnight, because you certainly aren't going to."

There was a brief silence as he sat there in his chair. There was a large window in the living room overlooking Lake Briscoe. The fire was crackling away in the fireplace. Snow had begun to fall, making the moment even more special. There was an aura of contentment about him. "Ted," he said after a moment, "the first thing you need to do is apologize to those kids when you see them on Monday."

"I beg your pardon?"

"In order to undergo complete transformation, you are going to have to apologize for the way you've treated your students," he said matter-of-factly.

"Yeah, but..."

"No 'Yeah-buts,' Ted. You're probably thinking to yourself these kids are the ones who owe you an apology, and I suppose in some ways you might be right. But you are the teacher, and it is your responsibility to improve the climate of your classroom. I'm afraid if you wait for them, you'll never get what it is you're looking for."

There was another brief silence. I knew he was right. Who was I kidding if I actually thought those kids would walk into my room on Monday and say, "Hey, Mr. C, I just want to apologize for the way I've been blowing you off this year. From this day forward, you will have my undivided attention. If for any reason I mess up, please give me a detention"?

He continued, "Ted, I know you have the tools within you to be not just a good teacher, but a great teacher." Slowing down just a bit, he said, "Every teacher goes through what you're going through. I went through it. Ruth Feely went through it." He paused for just a second and added somewhat under his breath, "And she never really came out of it."

We both laughed at that one.

"Hey, thanks for taking the time to talk with me," I said. "We should do this again sometime."

"Absolutely," he said, standing up with a big smile on his face. "Anytime you want to stop over and talk would be fine with me. Let's get together in a couple of weeks. Just give me a ten minute heads-up. I don't want you stopping by when I'm in my bathrobe, if you know what I mean."

"Good point," I replied. "Thanks again." Getting up to leave, I felt different. I felt good. For a brief while, my insides felt calm. I was at peace with myself and the situation staring me in the face.

Walking out into his entry way, he handed me my coat. "One last thing," he said before he closed the door behind me. "Nobody's got it totally figured out. It's only when people can admit they don't have it all together that they really begin to move in the right direction. You're on the right track, mister," he said with a grin. "Don't forget to take the first step when you get back on Monday."

During the remainder of my vacation, there was plenty of time to reflect on what Tim had said. The relationship that existed between myself and my students had been badly damaged. *By me.* It was my fault. I was the one who had become a dictator. It was my way or the highway. Why? Because I was scared of losing control, and in my fear, I had created the classroom climate I truly didn't want. As in any relationship, someone has to step up and practice humility. Knowing these kids wouldn't initiate left it up to me.

The remaining days of my holiday break went by without anything significant happening. Spending New Year's Eve by myself served only to remind me of how lonely I was.

The peace I felt in talking with Tim Fritz came to a screeching halt on the Sunday night before school was to resume. My nerves began square-dancing, as they often did, causing my stomach to tighten just a bit and my throat to constrict enough to make me feel uncomfortable, but not so much that I couldn't breathe. That just-got-kicked-in-the-gut feeling started to work its way through my body. That feeling of dread came over me where I almost wished something tragic would happen so I wouldn't have to stand in front of those kids and teach. A car accident would be perfect. Not enough to kill me; just enough to spend about a month in the hospital. Maybe when I got back, the kids would feel sorry for me, and maybe, just maybe, they'd behave themselves for once.

CHAPTER 9

Repentance

This first day back in early January had similar vibes to the first day of school in September. Two weeks off is a long time, and I wondered if I could remember all their names. With the bell only a few minutes away, my stomach began to feel heavy, and my throat felt tight. Inside, I wanted to cry. *"Nobody has it all figured out. It's only those people who can admit they don't have it all together who really begin to move in the right direction. You're on the right track."* Like a tiny shot of adrenaline, Tim Fritz's words reverberated around my head in those last few minutes before the kids came into the room. His words had a way of encouraging me. Thank goodness. I needed all the help I could get.

"Good morning, class," I said as they found their seats. "I hope you all had a good holiday vacation."

"Yeah, too bad we had to come back here," came Bryan's voice from the back of the room. *Ouch!* His comment was followed by many head nods and mumbles of agreement. It looked as though more than half the class felt the same way. The other kids were probably too polite to say anything.

This is going to be tougher than I thought. "Well, anyway...I'm glad you're here." Even coming out of my mouth, it felt strange. They sensed it as well. "Um...yeah," I continued. "Glad everyone here could make it today." *What in the world was I saying? Glad everyone here could make it today? What was that?*

I figured I better pull out of this nosedive before I said anything even more absurd. I proceeded. "Let's start by turning to page seventy-four in your grammar books." A few audible groans were heard throughout the room.

"Do we have to do grammar?" someone asked. "Man, we just got back. Can't we do something fun?"

"Now listen," I said. My blood pressure began its rapid ascent. My right armpit began heating up. Then suddenly, I stopped. "You know what? We're going to hold off on taking those books out for just a minute. There's something I need to do, and to be perfectly honest, this is something that's not going to be easy for me." There was a sudden silence, almost as if they were excited by the fact I was about to do something uncomfortable. They had watched me self-destruct countless times before, but never had I announced it ahead of time.

"This might sound kind of weird, but I.....owe...this class...an apology," I stuttered. *Don't expect things to be easy,* I heard Tim's voice echo in my mind. "I am going to be as honest with you as I possibly can right now." Waiting for my brain to catch up with my mouth, I continued, "This year has not gone the way I thought it would. And..." My brain began to short circuit. "And...I know that a lot of it...has..." My throat began to constrict even more as a huge lump rose from my chest and quickly settled into my throat. My eyes began to get blurry. *What the heck is going on here?!?!? Am I starting to cry?* Pausing to give my throat and eyes a chance to think about what they were doing, I continued, "I know that a lot of it... has to do with me."

At the exact millisecond those words left my mouth, a surge of relief and regret swept through every fiber of my body. *Should I be saying this?* The last thing I wanted to do was start boo-hooing in front of these kids. "I want to apologize for the way I've been responding to things around here. Now, before you get too excited, in no way am I letting this class off the hook for previous infractions. But I have failed miserably in my response to many of those situations."

I stopped for a moment to scan the crowd. They didn't look any different. There were still a few kids not really paying attention. Deep down, I was hoping for a little better reaction. For starters, it would have made me feel a lot better if they were all actually looking at me. Pete Hedler seemed to be fascinated by his pencil. I don't know what it is about those yellow number twos that just seem to mesmerize some kids. He was almost in a trance, rolling it between his index finger and thumb, looking rather intently at the very sharpened point. I wanted to walk over to him and say in an extremely sarcastic way, *"Fascinating, aren't they?"* At which point I would rip it out of his hand, hold it above my head and carry on in a mocking tone, *I wonder how they do it. How do they get that small piece of lead inside the pencil? Do they drill a hole in the piece of wood and then stick the lead through the center, or do they start with the lead and build the wood around it? I wonder if pencils and busses are painted with the same paint. Amazing, isn't it? Kind of makes you wonder what they'll come up with next, doesn't it?*

Nope. I wasn't going to do that. I wanted to do it (in a very bad way), but I knew better, and I decided to continue my apology. "The bottom line is…I haven't been as respectful as I should have been."

Looking up from the floor, I saw that some of the kids had a completely confused look on their faces, as if they'd never seen or heard an adult apologize before.

"I am going to commit to you, this day, to try and do a better job treating this class with the respect it deserves." Saying the last part was a little strange. At my core, I wasn't sure they deserved to be treated with respect, but I remembered what Tim had said during our afternoon chat: *You're the teacher; it's up to you to make the changes.*

Deep down, I wanted this moment to be monumental. To be that point in the year where everything turned around for the better. They would sense my regret, and out of pure kindness, they'd be better listeners. They'd treat people with respect. Especially me. I would take this class to new levels. New heights. Kids would thank me for being their favorite teacher. There'd be so much love and respect spewing out of these kids that we'd have to watch our step. There'd be no stopping us.

Judging by their empty stares, however, it was clear that all of what I had just said was still making its way from their eardrums to their brains. There was a brief silence, and then I figured we might as well get some work done.

Approximately four minutes transpired from the conclusion of my apology to the exact moment they were going to see if this change was for real.

I started by saying, "Okay, let's get back to those grammar books."

The words no sooner left my mouth when I heard a few groans. "Uh…wait a minute now." I paused for two reasons. One: to give my mouth and brain an opportunity to get on the same channel. Reason number two: try and stay calm. "Now as much as I'd love to just sit here and hang out with you and shoot the breeze all morning, we need to get some work done. The school board hired me specifically for the purpose of teaching you. Now when I say I'd love to just sit here and talk, I really would, but the powers-that-be are counting on me to make sure I do what they've hired me to do. So I need you to open your books to the next lesson."

"Do we have to do this? When are we ever going to use this stuff?" came Alex Gerard's voice from the middle of the room.

And then, all of a sudden, it was like a gift from God. Where normally I would have gotten upset and told him to do it because I said so and that was all the reason he needed, I very calmly replied, "Alex. You don't have to use this." I was a little surprised to hear these words come out of my mouth. And to be honest, I wasn't really sure what I was going to follow it up with. "You don't have to use any of the stuff I teach you. It's your choice whether or not you want to ignore the knowledge that lies within these books." Yup, this was definitely a gift from God, because there's no way I was smart enough to come up with that on my own, let alone have the guts to say it out loud.

I took a deep breath and continued, "I'm having you do this

lesson, Alex, because I care enough about you that I don't want you to sound like a hillbilly for the rest of your life when you talk to someone. Now, before you get upset and start thinking that I just called you a hillbilly, realize one thing: I didn't call you a hillbilly; I'm just doing my part to keep you from turning into one."

Some of the kids were smiling a little as I kept going. "You see, class, people aren't born hillbillies. They aren't born saying things like, '*Gawsh, Ma, you won't believe what I seen this morning when I was a-waiting for the bus. I seen a whole gob of deers in them there woods down by the river.*' No, it's my job to keep you from turning into a redneck hillbilly, and if I let you out of this assignment, you're going to be well on your way."

"But my uncle talks like that," little Ann Rosenthal squeaked.

"That's right," I said, having no idea who her uncle was or what he actually sounded like. "I'll bet his teachers let him get out of doing grammar. I'll bet he wishes he had your book right now so he could learn how to talk right." *Okay, I think I might have taken that one a little bit too far.* I didn't need her uncle showing up at my door in his grease-stained overalls with a sledgehammer resting against his shoulder, saying, "Are you that there teacher what wuz makin' fun of the way I talks? How would you like me to bust yore head?"

"All right, class. Let's get going on this assignment; I don't want you to have to take it home for homework tonight. You're going to have enough of that as it is."

"What!?!" they all shouted.

"I'm just kidding…kind of. Now, get going before I add more to it."

Later that day, I mixed it up during reading. Instead of having them do the same old thing they usually do (read the story, answer questions, turn it in, get it back, throw it away), I decided to try and give them something different. Instead of telling them what to do all the time, it was time to give them some options. Unfortunately, I hadn't thought through the choices very well. "Uh…would you like to read the odd pages or the…" I didn't even finish the sentence because I realized it didn't make sense. "Never mind. Tell you what…when you finish reading, you may either draw a picture that goes along with the story, or you can answer the questions at the end." *Whoa! That was close.* It wasn't what I imagined it to be like, but it was a start.

Later that week, I called Mr. Fritz after supper one night. In part to say thanks, but also to share some good news. Things had improved since we last met, mostly because of him. I also wanted to see if it was possible to get together again to talk about school. This man was a redwood of knowledge, and I, a lowly sapling, was in need of nourishment. His wisdom was like water and sunlight to me.

We met at The Oak Floor Inn for breakfast on Saturday morning. When Pam took our order, I almost asked for "The Binder," with its mountain of cheese and meat, but thought it best to play it safe for now. "I'll have two eggs over easy, American fries, no onions, and raisin toast," I told her.

"Anything to drink?"

"Just water," I said.

"How about it, Tim?" she asked when it was his turn.

My eyes almost bugged out their sockets when I heard him say, "Give me The Binder, Pam. I'm feeling pretty good today."

While we waited for our food, I talked. He listened. It was good to engage in a meaningful conversation, the thing I seemed to crave the most. Healthy dialogue. Two people using their time and energy on things that really mattered.

"You were right about one thing," I told him between bites of eggs and potatoes.

"What's that?" he asked.

"Change hasn't come easy," implying that things in my classroom had improved some.

He smiled over the rim of his coffee cup. "I know," he said. "I've been in your shoes before. But when you reach a point where you can look back and see growth, it's so rewarding." He took another hit of his coffee. "I believe in you, Ted. I know you can do it." His encouraging words landed like raindrops in the soft soil that was my heart.

His bright blue eyes sparkled in the early morning sunlight as we stood up, pushed in our chairs, and walked toward the exit. "Thanks, Tim," I said. "I really appreciate what you're doing for me."

"It's my pleasure," he said, smiling. "You're a great guy, Teddy," he said as we walked toward his car. He reached out to shake my hand. "Like I said before, anytime you want to get together, give me a call."

"Thanks again," I said, giving his hand one last squeeze.

As the weeks drifted by, I started using my time in the car to practice giving the kids in my class imaginary choices. I would think of a situation and then rehearse what I'd say. *You guys want to work quietly or silently?* Oooh…that was a good one. *Would you like to work by yourself or with a partner? Do you want to put that toy in your locker or in my desk?* It reached a point where it was kind of fun. I couldn't wait to get to school and try my new lines. One of my favorite moments came when three girls were whispering to each other at their group of desks while I was teaching at the front of the room. Through past experience and my interactions with Fritz, I knew yelling across the room wasn't going to be the most effective way to go about things. In an effort to be discreet, I casually walked back toward them. When I was right next to them, I crouched down and said in a voice just loud enough for them to hear, "You know, girls, I'm finding it kind of hard to concentrate with all the commotion going on back here. I understand your desire to socialize, but just so you know, when I get distracted, I don't do my best teaching, and I tend to get frustrated. When I get frustrated, I tend to make some really bad decisions. Decisions that will affect you." I lowered my voice even more, and for dramatic effect, I tilted my head forward while raising my eyebrows, "Can you help me out with this?" I questioned. They all nodded appropriately. This was actually more fun than yelling across the room. More rewarding too.

It was a step in the right direction. Slowly, but surely, I found myself enjoying bits and pieces of the day. Once during a math lesson, some boys were spinning a quarter. "Your pocket or mine?" I asked with just a little smile. Without a word, one of the boys quickly put it in his pocket. "Thanks, guys," I said with a wink and a thumbs up sign.

Another time, some girls were arguing about whatever it is girls argue about. "Girls," I said calmly, "right now I need you to get back to your assignment, but feel free to write a note to each other when you're done." I waited a moment, then said, "Don't forget to say something nice about your teacher too." They didn't think it was very funny, but I think I was on to something. I'd come to realize over the last few weeks that it was better for my class to think that I was a little bit weird than for them to think I was a mean, old ogre.

One thing that really seemed to help was allowing them the opportunity to work in small groups. Of course, I had realized long ago that the more I rambled on about something, the less interested they seemed. Taking into consideration that they had a strong desire to socialize, I gave them time to do things together, which seemed to improve the overall classroom climate.

There was one afternoon at school where I began to get almost giddy as I sensed an opportunity to try out one of my new lines. I'd rehearsed quite a bit in the car for this particular one, taking several days to get it just right. Then it happened. Ron Geizer walked up to me, stuck his completed assignment in my face, and said, "I'm done. Now what am I supposed to do?" This question drove me crazy for some reason. It was like they expected me to fill every second of the day for them. Like it was my job to make sure they never got bored.

"What do you want to do?" I asked him casually.

Then his face got all contorted, and he said, "Huh?"

I repeated the question, "What do you want to do?"

Finally he said, "I don't know."

"Well, let me know what you decide, and I'll let you know if it's okay."

He walked away with a completely befuddled look on his face. Twenty seconds later he came back and asked, "Can I read?"

Then, with absolute confidence, I said, "Sure, why not? That sounds like a good idea." As he walked back to his desk, I thought to myself, *They don't pay me enough to do all the thinking in here.*

Every moment of every day wasn't this relaxed. There were

definitely some times when I got a little upset. The old Ted Carter was still inside, at times trying to bust out. There were good days. There were bad days. At least the good moments were starting to outweigh the bad ones; it wasn't like earlier in the year when every moment of every day was flat out miserable. Maybe there is something to treating people with respect. Treating these kids with a little dignity seemed to be making a difference.

There were still times when someone would whine or complain about something. That's when I threw out my favorite line of all. "I can see this is important to you, but unfortunately, right now is not a good time. The only time I have to talk about this is after the last bell. Will that work for you?" With great delight I'd watch their eyes go from scorn to bewilderment. It was like a game of verbal judo, and I was actually scoring points.

Several weeks later, walking past the office one Friday morning in late winter, I looked through the office window at Carol. I had gotten in the habit of nodding my head in her direction if she happened to be looking up from her computer. Standing in front of her was the rear view of what could possibly be one of the most beautiful women I'd ever seen. Because I didn't want to get caught staring, I headed for the lounge. *Simmer down… Simmer,* I told myself. Though I didn't actually see her face, I had a gut feeling she was going to be pretty. Putting my lunch in the fridge, I checked the cupboards for nothing in particular. I was stalling. I wanted her to get in front of me so I could get an appropriate analysis as she walked down hallway. *Stay cool. Stay calm. Don't look too eager.* I tried to imagine what she'd look like. With the information I already had, *chestnut hair and…*well, I guess that was about it, I started putting her together in my head. Out of the corner of my eye, I noticed someone walk past the lounge. This was my chance. I walked through the door out into the main hallway.

"Hey, Carter," came a voice just off to my left. A man's voice. It was Gus Harble. "Check out the sub. She's hot." Though he made an attempt to whisper, it came out a little louder than is socially acceptable, almost like he'd learned how to whisper while riding in a helicopter.

"What?" I said, sounding just a little confused, but deep down my heart was playing hopscotch.

"Check out the sub," he said again. "Too bad I'm married," he went on.

Yeah right. I'm sure he's exactly what this girl wants to go out with. An arrogant, overweight, short, balding man with more hair coming out of his ears and nose than anyone would care to see.

"Yeah, that is too bad." *What a creep,* I thought.

That's when she walked out of the office. And that's exactly when I started to panic. She looked like the girl I'd seen at Gretchen's a few months ago. I just stared. Gus and I were both staring at her.

"Can one of you help me find Room Twelve?" she asked in a voice that reminded me of an angel.

I just stood there. Frozen. This *was* the girl from Gretchen's! Did she remember me? I wasn't sure if I wanted her to. She was probably thinking to herself, *Oh, you're that creepy guy who kept trying to stare at me, and then kept looking down at your plate every time I looked your way.*

"Sure, sweetie," came Gus's answer. "Keep on walking that way," he said, pointing down the hallway. "Third door on your left."

She looked at him like she wasn't quite sure what to make of him. I would have reached out to shake her hand, but mine was sweating so much. "I'm Ted," I said. But when I said "Ted," my voice cracked. She sort of smiled. I could feel my face burning.

"Nice to meet you, Ted," she said reaching out her hand. "I'm Sarah."

"Nice to meet you too," I said, wiping my hand on my pants as I reached out to shake hers. Her hands were beautiful. There's nothing I find more splendid than a female hand that's been well taken care of. Her delicate, soft hand sank into my cold, wet one, and I could see her start to smile again. Though it wasn't necessarily a pleasant smile. It was more of a smile that someone gives to help ease an awkward situation. Removing her hand from mine, I could see her discreetly brush it across the side of her pants. *Real nice. I've just grossed out one of the nicest-looking girls I've met in a long time.*

I found myself thinking about her quite a lot that morning.

During silent reading time, I pretended to browse through a magazine. I wasn't even looking at the words; I was just thinking about Sarah. Even though I had a ton of papers sitting on my desk waiting to be corrected, I didn't feel like doing it then.

"Hey, Mr. C," I heard someone shout. "Are we going to lunch today?"

Looking up at the clock, I noticed it was five minutes past the time we usually left to go down to the cafeteria. "Yes, yes, it is time for lunch," I said. "Let's hurry up; I don't want anyone to miss their precious lunch time." I was so excited to see this new beauty who for most of the morning had been occupying my thoughts. I secretly hoped she wasn't dating anyone, or even worse, what if she was married?

After taking my class to the cafeteria, I walked into the teachers' lounge and noticed her sitting at the opposite end of the table where I normally sat. I glanced around the room. There were two seats available next to her, as well as the seat at the other end of the table, my normal lunch spot. I made a snap decision. I sat down right next to her. I didn't care what anyone thought. Hopefully, I wasn't being too obvious.

"Yo, Ted...why are you sitting down there today? Your seat is right here," Gus said with an obvious smirk on his face.

"Uh..." My face started to burn immediately. "Uh...I just thought I'd like to try a different seat today."

"*Okay,*" he said in the most sarcastic tone.

What a ding-dong, I thought. His life was so miserable he had to do this kind of stuff to brighten his day.

My whole lunch period was spent listening to Sarah talk with Fran Helman, one of our first grade teachers. I could tell that she wasn't really interested in what Fran was saying. Fran was going on and on about her husband's honeybees. Fran was looking for a sale. I was looking for this girl's left hand. When she took a bite of her sandwich, I found the answer. No wedding ring. *Yes!!* Always the first step when looking for a suitable companion.

"Where ya' from?" Gus asked, interrupting Fran's sales pitch for honey.

"I grew up in Hollisford," she said.

I almost choked on my lunch. *Hollisford? This girl was from Hollisford?* How come I've never seen her before? *Hollisford?* I decided not to hold that against her.

The rest of lunch went by way too quickly. Just being in her presence, combined with the idea of something happening, left me feeling giddy. There's nothing quite like the feeling of hope that accompanies a new relationship. Especially when the other person is attractive. There was a new spring in my step after that. I didn't really do a lot of teaching the rest of the day. I assigned a lot of independent seat work, allowing myself time to plan my next move with Sarah.

I knew there was no chance of the school catching on fire and me running back in to rescue her.

"Oh, Ted, I'm so glad you came back for me," she'd say.

"How can I ever repay you?" she'd ask with a deep sense of longing in her eyes.

"It was nothing," I'd tell her. *"If you're looking for a way to make things right, though, how about you and me going out for dinner this Saturday?" I'd say with all the confidence I could muster. She'd say yes, and we'd get married over the summer. I started thinking about where we could go on our honeymoon and what kind of house we'd live in, how many children...*

Because I'm such a big chicken when it comes to asking women out, I thought about drinking a few beers, chasing her down in the parking lot, and saying, "Hey, baby, you want to go out sometime?" But drinking alcohol on school property is not a good idea.

"Yo, Mr. C, are you going to let us leave today? It's time to go," a voice hollered from somewhere in the back row.

"Oh, yeah. Sure. Um... have a good weekend, everybody." I stood up from behind my desk and just for fun, I decided to high-five the students on their way out. They didn't all reciprocate, but it felt good making an effort.

Sarah happened to be walking out of the school at the same time I was.

"Um...how long have you been subbing?" I asked, saying the first thing that came to my mind.

"This is my first time. I just finished my student-teaching last fall in a little district near Grand Rapids. My boyfriend and I were supposed to get married last summer, but..." She paused for a second. "But things didn't work out," she finally said.

"Oh...I'm sorry." Though looking at her, I wasn't sorry at all. If anything, I was elated. We both got in our separate vehicles, and as I watched her drive out of the parking lot, my heart began to jiggle with excitement at the thought of possibly asking her out.

She consumed my thoughts for much of the weekend. In my mind, I was a lot more valiant and courageous than real life. What's so hard about asking someone out? What's the worst thing that could happen? When I played through the imaginary situations in my head, the risks seemed worth it. I knew better, though. If she were standing right here in front of me, I was almost certain I wouldn't have the guts to go through with it. Every girl I had ever dated had been the one to ask me out. While that was okay then, that's not really how I wanted things to go down this time.

In a stroke of good luck, Sarah ended up subbing quite a bit in Coleman. Specifically for Helen McGinnis, one of the more *seasoned* teachers at school. Helen was going to retire after this year, so she felt it was her duty to use as many sick days as she could before her time ran out. Most of these so-called sick days came on Fridays and Mondays. A month ago I saw Helen on a Friday night at Gretchen's after one of her *supposed* sick days. "How you feeling?" I asked when I saw her.

"Fine," she said with a tinge of impertinence. After that, there wasn't anything to say, and feeling more than a little awkward, I just went and sat down somewhere else.

Then Helen decided to have some minor surgery performed on her foot, and she wanted to have it done while her insurance was still in effect, so she called on Sarah to fill in for her short-term leave. While most people would have been able to come back after a day or two, Helen insisted she would need at least two weeks to make a full recovery. Having Sarah in the building for an extended period made me secretly hope Helen never came back.

Sarah's two weeks of subbing seemed to go faster than

usual. She had a quiet calm about her that really put me at ease. Sometimes we found ourselves talking at lunch, and occasionally, we'd spend time talking in the hallway after school. If it hadn't been for the presence of other staff members, our shared moments kind of felt like being on a date. After a while, I noticed our conversations were starting to occur more frequently, and I seriously wondered if there were any other possible surgeries Helen might want to consider.

On her last afternoon filling in for Helen, as the last student left for the day, I planned my big move with Sarah. I quickly shut the door to my room and turned off the lights. Without even thinking, I peeled off twelve and a half push-ups as a way to alleviate the angst building inside me. My goal was twenty, but I could tell at eleven that wasn't going to happen. I had all this energy inside of me, and I knew what I had to do. I was going to ask Sarah out on a date. Even though I had no idea what I would do if she said yes, I didn't want to lose this opportunity. Too many times I'd missed out on things because I failed to take a risk. I didn't want to sit around all weekend wishing I'd said or done something.

I started walking down the hall toward her room. My walk turned into an accelerated gallop as I got closer.

Walking up to the doorway of Helen's classroom, anticipation had escalated into full-fledged gaiety as my eagerness hit the boiling point. Upon reaching her room, my heart hit the floor. The door was closed. The lights were off. She was gone. Immediately, my brain went to the worst possible scenario: She'd never sub at our building again.

A week later, however, she subbed for Gus. It was clear from the looks on the kids' faces that they were more than a little glad to have a reprieve from Mr. Harble. Some of the boys were making gestures and facial expressions that clearly indicated they were going to be paying very close attention today. Not because the content would be any more interesting—just the person delivering it. Jealousy quickly set in. *Slow down a second,* I thought. *If she's interested in twelve and thirteen year old boys with all their greasy hair and pimpled faces, then I probably don't want to hang out with her anyway.* Almost as if Ms. Horter had come back from the grave, I told myself, *Simmer. Simmer.*

"Have you found everything you need?" I asked, popping my head into Gus's classroom, secretly hoping she would need some help with *something.*

"Do you know where he keeps the teacher's edition of his math book?" she asked. "I can't find it anywhere."

We both looked in the obvious places. Under piles of worksheets he kept on the counter behind his desk.

"Math isn't my strong suit," she said with a grin. "I majored in English."

Math wasn't my strong suit either, but before I could stop the words from leaving my mouth, I blurted, "I know a thing or two about math. Tell you what. I'll take a copy of these problems with me, and I'll have an answer key for you before 9:30."

My major was geography, so promising to help her out put me in a little bit of a bind. After finding two eighth grade boys who looked fairly smart, I agreed to give them each a bottle of Coke if they had the answers back on my desk before 9:20. They were back by 9:15. "Are you sure these are right?" I asked skeptically.

"Absolutely," one of them replied. "We did this same sheet for Mr. Harble last year."

"Thanks, guys," I said. "You'll have your Cokes by the time lunch rolls around."

They seemed pleased and were soon on their way.

"I got those answers for you," I said as I walked back to Gus's room.

"Oh, thank you," she said. "I owe you one."

My first thought was, *How about going out with me on Saturday?* Before that thought got any closer to my mouth, I quickly said, "No problem; it was nothing."

At the end of the day, walking past Gus's room, I saw her sitting at the huge wooden desk that Gus often sat behind. She was looking down, obviously writing up her review of the day's events. I kept walking. Having no particular place to go, I stopped, counted to ten and started walking back the other way toward her. My heart rate increased. My right armpit started to tense up. I knocked on the window to the room and slowly walked in. "So...how'd it go today?" I asked.

"Oh, not too bad," she said, followed by a few seconds of silence. "Your answer key for math was very much appreciated."

Without thinking, I said, "Anytime you need me to lend a hand, I'm more than willing." Instantly, my face turned red. Trying to ease the awkwardness created by my comment, I asked, "Well, uh... do you think you might be able to sub for me sometime?" *Now that was clever.*

"Sure. That would be great. I'd like that."

"Cool. Can I get your number?"

"What?" she asked.

"Uh....yeah...your number so I can call you if I need a sub."

"Oh, sure," came her reply. She looked almost relieved that I wasn't planning to ask her out. She scribbled down her seven digit phone number and held it out to me. Right before I took it, though, she snatched it back and began writing something else. It wasn't just one or two words either. Once she finished, she folded the paper twice and handed it to me.

"Here you go," she said with a smile that just about melted my heart. My insides quivered like a tuning fork. Because of the extra excitement, I felt my guts loosen, and I just wanted to stand there and look at her forever.

My heart was doing somersaults as I walked out to my car. *Oh my word. I can't believe she just gave me her number.* As I approached the car, it dawned on me that if I was home *sick* and she was subbing, I wouldn't see her at all. Oops.

Once I climbed into the driver's seat and shut the door, I slowly unfolded the crumpled piece of notebook paper. Slowly I read her number out loud, and then, to my heart's desire, I read what she had added...*Don't wait until you're sick to call!*

CHAPTER 10

Everyone's Got a Story

The thought of calling Sarah was more than I could stand. Nervousness and excitement were like tectonic plates pushing against each other. When I thought about being with her, I was ecstatic. When I thought about picking up the phone and dialing her number to ask her out, I could feel supper contemplating a return trip up my esophagus.

Because I had not yet asked the big question, here I was again on Friday night, spending another evening with my folks. Listening to their banter should have been enough incentive to get off my rear end, socially speaking. Here was yet another night of watching the news, followed immediately by *Wheel of Fortune* and *Jeopardy* with my parents. If they were actual contestants on *Jeopardy*, they'd owe the show money. My mother consistently enters final jeopardy with anywhere from negative three thousand to negative ten thousand. My dad only answers the questions he knows for sure, which is one or two per show. I'm the only one making a profit once in a while. If I had been an actual contestant last Tuesday, I would have walked away with thirty-five hundred dollars. Sure, it was imaginary money, but it was good enough for second place. Rarely do I ever get final jeopardy correct. Had I stayed in college for another four years, maybe I'd do better.

My mom and dad have more of a hankering for *Wheel of Fortune*. My mom gets more correct answers than on *Jeopardy*, and my dad likes watching Vanna White flip the letters.

At the end of *Jeopardy,* I decided to call Clip and see what he was doing. We decided to meet at Gretchen's for no particular reason other than to not be at home.

On the way into town, my thoughts went back to when Clip and I were younger. We used to do everything together, but once we graduated high school and I went off to college, things changed. It was hard to maintain the relationship when there was more than an hour's drive between us.

Pulling up to the curb in front of Gretchen's, I waited a few minutes before getting out. His car was nowhere to be seen, and to avoid looking like a total loser sitting at a table by myself, I waited until he showed up.

"How's school?" he asked later as we sat down at the bar.

I replied, "Not too bad. It's getting better, I suppose. Probably too late in the year to get another snow day. " *Did I just say that out loud?* Though it's not uncommon to get snow in these parts well into April.

"I know what you mean. Things have been pretty slow at the lumberyard lately. Not a lot of construction going on right now."

In the back of my mind, I realized Clip and I were growing apart. He didn't really know what I meant when I said I'd like another snow day. School and Larry's Lumber were worlds apart. We weren't as close as we used to be. We were two different people, moving in very different directions. We only got together if *I* called. He never picked up the phone to see what I was doing or ask if I wanted to get together.

I was tempted to interrupt him in mid-sentence and say something along the lines of "Well, Clip. It's been a good run. We had some good times, you and me. I'm sorry it has to end like this. Good luck in everything." No, we just sat there talking about nothing in particular. Getting up and walking out not only would have been extremely rude, but that would also be a great source of uneasiness, as Coleman isn't that big. The chances of seeing him around town were pretty high. It was kind of sad to think that I was winding down with one of my best friends of all time. I wondered if he sensed the same thing. Basically, we were still hanging around because we didn't have anyone else. Never a good sign.

"Have you gotten a date with Kim Busche yet?" he asked out of nowhere.

"No, not yet, but I'd be happy to put in a good word for *you*."

"That's all right," he said. "She may be a little out of my league. Really hot women don't usually go for plain, ordinary guys who work in lumberyards."

"Oh, I don't know, she might be getting desperate," I said, slugging his shoulder. "But if things *did* work out between the two of you, I know one thing for sure."

"What's that?" he asked.

"You'd definitely be seeing less of me."

"Why's that?"

"Because," I replied, "she hasn't changed much since high school. She's only gotten worse. She's still fairly good-looking, it's just too bad her personality never caught up. She's so full of herself." As the words left my mouth, I felt bad about what I was saying. Still, it didn't stop us from carrying on the conversation.

"What a shame," he said, "to have that much beauty and never be able to use it."

"No kidding. Too bad we couldn't combine her looks with some of the more unattractive girls from our class. You know—the ones who actually have an ounce of humility."

"I don't know about you," Clip said, "but I'd be willing to give my left arm to go out with someone soon. No offense, but you just don't meet all my needs." The smirk on his face was enough for me to know that he was kidding. But he was right.

We left Gretchen's around eleven o'clock. As we walked out to our cars, I said, "See you around."

"Yeah, take care, man," he replied.

Sitting down in the driver's seat, I slowly closed the door and waited a moment before putting the key in the ignition. I liked Clip.

I was thankful for what we had. I wasn't ready to give up on him yet, though I think we both knew our good times together had peaked long ago.

When I got home, my mom and dad were both sleeping. My father was in his recliner wearing his *tighty-whiteys* and a bathrobe with a half eaten bowl of popcorn sitting on his lap. If history was any indicator, that was probably his fourth or fifth bowl. My mom was lying on the sofa with a magazine draped across her chest. The TV was still on. Apparently, it wasn't loud enough to keep them awake. *Is this what I have to look forward to? Am I going to reach a point where I work all week, looking forward to the weekend, only to waste most of it sleeping on the couch in front of the TV?* It seemed like they were missing out on life. The rest of the world was doing its thing, but Marvin and Noreen Carter seemed oblivious to it all. Tomorrow would be another Saturday with them floating around the house, staying busy but never really accomplishing anything worthwhile. My father tends to stay outside or in the garage, while my mother finds things to do inside like moving her knick-knacks from one place to another.

There was a part of me that wanted to wake them up and tell them that I had met a very nice girl at school, but I was certain they would only feign minor enthusiasm and then go back to sleep.

When I was in high school, my brother once mentioned that he liked a girl and wanted to ask her out on a date. Instead of being happy for him, my dad asked him if he would pass the meatloaf. After a while, you stop sharing significant moments with people for fear that whatever is on *their* mind is more important than what's on yours. And then it hit me. I realized I had done that very same thing to my students earlier this year. The wave of regret was quickly replaced by one of gratitude. I replayed what Tim had said earlier: *When you reach a point where you can look back and see growth, it's so rewarding.* The corners of my mouth moved into a short, small smile. Looking at my parents sprawled out on the living room furniture, I knew what else I needed to do. Stop being so critical. Maybe there was more to these two people than what I saw from the outside. Maybe I just needed to look a little deeper.

I've always loved Saturday mornings. Nothing is quite as sweet as having no responsibility. Lying there in bed with nothing but time. I could hear my dad in the kitchen making his breakfast. How one man can make that much clatter for a bowl of oatmeal is beyond me.

I started to think about Sarah. I barely knew her, but the deep longing I had to spend time with her was getting more intense every day. Looking out my bedroom window, I gazed at the tip of the old maple tree in our backyard. The deep blue sky painted behind it was a beautiful backdrop. There were tiny buds beginning to grow on the finger-like branches. The buds represented new life. They would become dark green leaves in a few weeks. They reminded me a bit of myself. I too had a new lease on life. Thanks in large part to Tim Fritz. I wondered if God had planned for me to run into him over winter vacation at Glen's, or whether it was just a stroke of good luck. Thinking back on my days as an undergraduate, I shook my head, realizing how little I knew back then. Yet for some strange reason, I thought I had it all together. Tim's words circled my brain in a soothing, calming manner: *Nobody has it all figured out. It's only when people can admit they don't have it all together that they really begin to move in the right direction.*

I don't think it was just plain luck that brought the two of us together. Divine intervention is more likely. It began to dawn on me that without the disappointments and failures of the past few months, I would probably be the same Ted Carter I was a year ago. Someone full of angst and uncertainty. Was it possible that God had lined things up in such a way to help me reach this point? A point where a small ember of hope was flickering off in the distance, calling my name, encouraging me to have faith that everything was going to turn out just fine? One thing was for certain. I never would have reached it on my own.

I leaned over the side of my bed, reached into my pants pocket, and pulled out Sarah's number. I closed my eyes, thinking of what it would be like to pick her up on a date and take her somewhere special. I'd had girlfriends before, but I couldn't think of anything that I'd done that was really spectacular. Some people have these fascinating stories about their first dates. Airplane rides. Spectacular sunsets. I was drawing a blank. Maybe she didn't need spectacular. Maybe she'd be happy with someone who wasn't out to impress her. Maybe she'd enjoy meaningful conversation more than an impressive activity.

Reaching up on top of my headboard, I grabbed the phone and dialed her number...except for the last digit. I immediately put the phone back on the receiver. My heart was racing like mad, and my hands were sweating. Again, I dialed the number. All the numbers. The phone rang.

"Hello," came a deep, husky voice.

I was so nervous, I said just about the dumbest thing possible. "Uh...hello...is this Sarah?" I managed to ask. *What on earth was I saying? Of course it wasn't Sarah. Get it together, Carter!* "I mean, is Sarah there?" I quickly asked.

"Sure. Hold on a second," came the voice that obviously belonged to her father. There was a long silence, and after a few minutes I heard a faint voice in the background ask, "Who is it?" I didn't hear anything after that. I assume her father probably shrugged his shoulders or something.

After a few seconds, I heard her say, "Hello."

Then, without really thinking...again, I skipped the small talk and just blurted out, "Um...this is Ted Carter. I was calling to see if you'd like to go out sometime."

Silence.

"Sure," she said.

"Great." At this point, due to my heart palpitations and shortness of breath, one syllable words were all I could gather. There was an awkward pause as I searched for what to say next. "Uh...well, I'll give you a call next week then." As soon as it came out, I knew how ridiculous it sounded. "I mean, I'll give you a call so we can set something up." This was getting worse by the second. "So, I'll talk to you later."

"O…kay," she said with a trace of uncertainty, followed by nervous laughter.

"Bye."

"Bye." And then the phone clicked. On one hand, I was glad that part was over, even though I sounded like a total moron. On the other hand, I now had to think of something to do.

Later that afternoon, I grabbed my guitar and went over to Grandma's. She mentioned a few days ago that she'd like to hear me play. She loved the old hymns. "Amazing Grace" and "How Great Thou Art" were her favorites. I sat in the living room, plucking away, while she went in and out of different rooms doing this and that. "Those songs remind me of your grandpa," she said, sitting down on the couch. "He loved those songs so much. He didn't cry very often, but there were times I would look over at him in church, and he'd be all teary-eyed. They weren't tears of sorrow. They were genuine tears of joy. Your grandpa felt those songs on a deep level, Teddy. I miss him every day." Her eyes began to glisten too as she reflected on the memory of her beloved husband. "I want you to know something," she said looking directly in my eyes. "Your grandpa and I prayed for you and Thad every day." She just sat there looking at me before adding, "Of course, it's just me now…" She didn't finish the sentence, but I had a pretty good idea of how it would have ended.

There were words swirling around inside my head, but none that seemed appropriate to say out loud. Looking back into her eyes, I simply pursed my lips together and gave a few quick nods, as if to say, "Thanks for sharing that with me."

"There's a tremendous amount of power in prayer," she continued, reaching over to put her hand on my arm. "We don't always see the results right away, but I'm telling you, Teddy, there is power in prayer."

Though she spoke plainly, her words left me feeling challenged and encouraged at the same time, almost as if she was passing on the most priceless piece of wisdom she had, and it was in my best interest to start applying it in my own life. As the silence inched forward, I looked away and began to slowly slide my thumb and forefinger over the strings, allowing their vibrations to once again fill the air.

I knew I had something special with my grandma. There was an appreciation I felt way down deep. Sitting there strumming my guitar, I was immersed in thankfulness for the opportunity to spend time with her. Without giving it much thought, I asked, "What time should I pick you up for church tomorrow?"

"Be here at 8:30," she said, giving me a smile.

When I was younger, I used to go to church every Sunday with my grandpa and grandma. It was something I looked forward to. As I got older, it was easy to make excuses for not going. My grandma had this peace about her, and I guess I thought by going to church with her again, maybe I could get in on it.

The next day, after listening to a sermon that focused primarily on forgiveness, I took Grandma to The Oak Floor Inn for lunch. Just me and her. After stuffing myself full of salad and bread sticks, our meals arrived. Most of mine went home in a Styrofoam container, as there wasn't much room left in my stomach.

After dropping her off at home, I found myself pulling into the school parking lot. Based on what I'd heard earlier at church, there was something I felt compelled to do. Getting out of my car, approaching the glass double doors, I felt an element of anxiety creep over me. Fumbling with my keys, I finally found the right one and opened the door. Stopping for a moment, I listened to them clank shut behind me. It was dark and deathly quiet. The familiar hum of fluorescent lighting was nonexistent. It was too quiet. Almost spooky. Like a blind man, I navigated my way down the hallway to my room. Once inside, I turned the lights on and walked up to the front of the room. Staring out at the sea of desks, I zeroed in on a few in particular. One of them belonged to Bryan Brookens. It was easy to find his desk. There were tiny pieces of paper, pencil shavings, and ground-up bits of eraser all over the floor underneath it. I was almost afraid to touch it, as numerous sheets of paper and textbooks were on the verge of falling out.

I slowly walked over to his desk and laid my hand on the top. Then I closed my eyes. I stood there for a minute just thinking about this kid who had driven me nuts for so long. And then I prayed for him. It felt weird, but I prayed that this kid would somehow be able to make it in life. It wasn't a long or fancy prayer. Right to the point. "God, I hope this kid makes it." I felt obligated to add a little more. "And …if there's any way you can use me…" I stopped again. I knew how I felt, but at the time, it was difficult to articulate my emotions.

Standing there in the middle of my empty classroom, with my hand on Bryan Brookens' desk, I asked God to forgive me for the way I'd treated him and this class. Like a giant wave crashing against a rock, a quiet peace began to swell over me. Then, I slowly went around to all the other desks, placing my hand on the smooth wooden tops of each one and quietly saying a small prayer for every kid in my room.

Lying in bed that night, the knot that had worked its way into my gut every Sunday night was gone. My eyes began to get stingy and wet, but I didn't care. It felt good to cry. With my eyes still damp, I drifted off into a most peaceful sleep.

The next week flew by. The kids were amazing. It was like an alien spaceship had landed in Coleman, sucked up all my students, then spit out brand new kids with kind hearts and willing attitudes. They listened. They got along. We laughed. We talked. Everything that *could* go right, went right. Some of my students even told me I was doing a great job. *Wow.* Then came the part I'd been desperately waiting for all week… Saturday night.

I met Sarah at her home. I had decided we would drive to Rosebush, the next town over, for a bite to eat. Taking a girl to a restaurant in a town where everyone knows you is not the best way to approach a first date. The whole time we ate, I'd be worried that someone would see us. Not because I was embarrassed of Sarah, mind you; it's just that I didn't want to try and explain things. I just wanted to get to know her and not be bothered by people. We went to Rosebush and ate at Rusty's Roadhouse. Their salad bar is outstanding. I panicked just a little when I thought I saw a kid from school, but it ended up being someone else. One of the highlights was when she reached across the table and wiped some ranch dressing from the corner of my mouth. WITHOUT

A NAPKIN!!! She used her bare hand. Those soft, delicate fingers touched my face! The rest of the meal was a blur. I could tell she thought I was funny. On the way home, she reached over and held my hand. I couldn't stand it. I love it when girls make it easy for you. The only thing better would be to have a mind reader telling me what she was thinking.

I hope he kisses me when he drops me off at home, she'd be thinking to herself. I'd smirk as the mind reader fed me useful information. I'd draw out the intensity as long as I could. Knowing that she wanted me to kiss her would be so cool. Walking her up the steps to her front door, I'd say, "I don't usually kiss on the first date, but for some reason I'm finding myself wanting to end this night right." Her eyes would flutter; she'd blush just a little. I'd lean in, stopping for a moment to look into her eyes, before proceeding the rest of the way.

BEEP, BEEP, BEEP, BEEP!!!!

It was my alarm clock. *What the heck!!!!* It had all been a dream. The perfect class. The perfect date. All a dream. I immediately hit the snooze button in an effort to fall back asleep and pick up where I had left off. No luck.

That "Monday-morning-feeling" that normally swept over me was gone. Even though I felt better, it was still tough to get out of bed in the morning, knowing I had a full week ahead. However, I knew I couldn't stay in the warm coziness too long. Then, something magical happened. Something only teachers can experience. The phone rang.

"Hello?"

It was Carol Carroll, the school secretary. "No school today," she said matter-of-factly. "Go back to bed."

"What?"

"Six inches of snow, Ted. No school."

"All right. Thanks." I hung up the phone. I felt my insides loosen even more. *Holy cow! What a gift. No school.* I remember getting this kind of news when I was younger. But the feeling I had then was nothing compared to right now. I did manage to go back to sleep, but there was no continuation of my dream.

Later, I sat at the kitchen table eating my breakfast. It was 10:36. Normally I'd be at school right now trying to get my class to listen to me. I sat there thinking about them.   Sitting there, I just thought about being a teacher. What an awesome responsibility.   Parents trusted me with their children. Not something to take lightly. Not having children of my own, it was difficult to grasp fully what that meant, but I knew it was important. I thought about my first day. Thank goodness every day wasn't that stressful.   I thought about Bryan Brookens again and how he used to drive me crazy. (And sometimes still did.) I thought about how he was never sick. *Why is it that the kids who challenge us the most are never gone?* I thought about inventing a can of flu spray. I'd be in my classroom pretending to spray air freshener. Then I'd walk right over to Bryan and cover him with it. Three or four days without him would be fantastic.

Instantly, I felt bad. Why would I want to do that? The old Ted would love to spray influenza over his class. The new Ted would only think about it, laugh, and move on. I couldn't quite put my finger on what was happening inside of me, but deep down, I kind of liked it. I was at a point where I could look back to the beginning of the year and see small areas of growth. And that felt good. Even though it was probably the hardest, roughest period of my life, somehow I felt stronger. I felt wiser. A little bit older, too. Maybe not so much in years, but in some other realm. I looked out the kitchen window at the remains of a late season snowstorm; the blanket of white snow covered the trees and grass. The robins were flitting to and fro, desperately seeking shelter from the cold.

I gave Tim Fritz a call later in the morning. We met for lunch at Gretchen's. He asked me how things were going at school.

"Better," I told him. I found myself wanting to soak up all the knowledge I could from this guy. He wasn't preachy. He had a way of telling me what I needed to hear without the *holier-than-thou* attitude.

Later in the meal, he hit me right between the eyes with some very powerful words. "You know, Ted," he said to me, "one of the most important things I've learned through teaching is that everyone has a story." I must have looked a little confused because he continued, "In other words, every single person you encounter, whether it's one of your students, a family member, or even one of your friends, has so much more going on inside them than you'll ever know. But once you get to know a person, once you get to know their story, you'll be amazed at how much you like them. Once the external layers are peeled away, you'll begin to understand that we all struggle and wrestle with a lot of the same things, and once you realize *that*, it makes a huge difference in how you relate to people."

There was a brief pause before he continued, "Those kids in your class need to know your story too, Ted. They need to know who you are, because they can't love somebody they don't know." He picked up his napkin and quickly wiped his hands and face. Setting it on the table, he went on to say, "That doesn't mean you spill your guts every time you're having a bad day. It just means you need to let them in on your life a little bit, so they get to know you. Once they realize you're a real person with feelings, they can't help but fall in love with you. And if they love you, they'll do anything for you."

The stuff he told me was so *common sense*, so easy to understand, yet in the back of my mind, I knew I wouldn't have reached these conclusions on my own. Sitting there at the table across from Tim, realizing what an honor it was to be in his company, a feeling of gratitude enveloped my existence, a feeling that made me want to change even more. To be someone who cared about kids and other people too. Not an ornery, stubborn guy who allowed situations and circumstances to dictate his feelings.

It was easy to be optimistic when we were together. He had such a positive way of offering suggestions. He never once said, "You need to do *this* or *that*." It was more like, "You might want to try..." or "What do you think about...." It put me at ease and made me want to listen. Knowing he had gone through similar situations made it much easier to listen.

Picking his coffee cup off the table, he took a quick sip before adding, "When I remember that every person has a story, it reminds me to treat them with respect and dignity...even if they're hard to like."

When someone says something like that, it's best just to be quiet and let it soak in. Saying anything at all would only take away from the experience. A quick nod or two of the head is about the only appropriate response.

Then he hit me again. "Words are funny," he said quietly. "We only seem to remember the ones that hurt us or help us."

Driving home from lunch gave me time to reflect on Tim's words of wisdom. I thought of Bryan Brookens and how I hated him so much at the beginning of the year. I thought about his story, how he had been neglected, abused, and abandoned by his parents. He had real wounds that needed to be healed, not have salt rubbed into them by some guy on a power trip.

I wondered about people like Gus Harble and Kim Busche. Could this stuff apply to them as well? Tuning the radio dial to WKIL, I found that the hard rock sounds vibrating around the interior of my car helped drive home the lesson I had just learned.

Lying in bed that night, I allowed my newfound wisdom to seep a little deeper. It's those quiet moments, when we're all alone, that we're most receptive to the voice in our heads. My brain felt like a hamster on a wheel. All this information was running around, waiting for my mind to settle down before it would sink into the folds of my brain.

I could hear the TV in the living room and the sound of my parents snoring. Lying on my back in the quiet that filled my room, I realized what a wiener I'd been at times toward my mom and dad. I had taken my parents for granted. Instead of being thankful for the things they had done for me over my lifetime, I'd focused more on their faults. My parents had stories, too. Each of them was shaped by the things that happened to them.

I thought about my dad and how he fought to graduate from high school, and how his dad left home when he was just a young kid of seven or eight. Things like that tend to leave scars. Despite having slight dyslexia and being held back in sixth grade, he worked his tail off in order to don a cap and gown and walk across the stage of the high school gymnasium with a diploma in his hand.

My mom had her story too. Losing her twin sister in an automobile accident when they were seventeen had left a huge hole in her heart. To lose not only a sister but a best friend, that was something I couldn't even imagine.

Instead of being an ungrateful son who took his parents for granted, maybe I could show them some appreciation. Instead of being a horse's rear end, maybe I could show them the respect they deserved. Lying there in the dark, quiet stillness of my room, I was glad Tim Fritz had helped me realize what really matters in life. I was glad I hadn't resigned. I was glad to have an opportunity to make some changes, and in turn, make a difference...for the better.

Waking up on Tuesday morning felt different. I realized there was hope. Hope for me. Hope that I could stand in front of a bunch of sixth graders and truly have them believe in me. And...maybe I could believe in them too.

Right before school started, as the kids were coming in from outside, Bryan turned away from his locker and approached the classroom. I did something very unusual. Especially for me. I stuck out my hand.

"Good morning, Bryan." He looked at my hand like it was coated with leprosy. "Good morning," I said again. He stuck his hand out and weakly shook mine. It felt weird. Then I proceeded to shake hands with every student entering my classroom. Some of them shook my hand with complete confusion. Others, mostly the boys, took advantage of the opportunity to squeeze my hand as hard as they could. I'm guessing they were still holding a grudge from the way the *old* Mr. Carter treated them.

"Good morning, class," I said as they sat down. "Take out your homework from last night, please."

"Why did you shake our hands this morning?" Pete Hedler asked.

"Oh, I don't know. It just seemed like a nice thing to do."

"O...kay," he said slowly.

Another student raised her hand. "Are you going to be doing

that every day?"

"I don't know. I may. I just thought shaking your hand was a better way to start the day than just telling you to take out your homework."

"I think the best way to start the day," Rudy Teigan said, "is to NOT go over the homework. Let's pretend you forgot about it."

"Well, I understand your situation, Rudy, but I don't think the school board would appreciate me not giving you homework." One of the things Fritz had taught me was to deflect the responsibility in certain situations. "Put the blame on the school board or the principal," he had told me. "That way, you don't look so bad." He laughed when he told me this, and we both knew it was kind of a joke, but I was thankful for the opportunity to put it into practice.

"I won't tell," he said with a huge grin.

This may not seem like a huge deal, but just *talking* felt good. Maybe my students liked it too. Then I had another idea.

"Before we start," I said, "I'd like to just take a minute or two to give you the opportunity to share with us something that's going on in your life. If there's something really cool happening, and you feel comfortable enough to share it with us, I want to give you the opportunity."

"Does it have to be something related to school?" Ron Geizer asked.

"Not at all," I replied. "As a matter of fact, I'd like to steer you in the direction of sharing something that maybe most of us don't know. Is there anyone who would like to begin?"

Burt Flanagan raised his hand. "Yes, Burt."

"Um, last night my mom and dad took me out for dinner."

"That's cool, Burt. Where'd you go?"

"We went to Rusty's Roadhouse."

"That's great. Well, thanks for sharing." Ew... that made me think about my dream. *Perhaps I better plan on going somewhere else,* I thought. "Does anyone else have something to share?" A silence fell over the room. Then, sounding much like the teacher in *Ferris Bueller's Day Off,* I said, "Anyone... anyone?"

Old Memories

On the way home from school, I decided to drop by Grandma's house, maybe grab a little something to eat. As I walked in through the front door, she looked up from the newspaper. The flier for Glen's was open on the table.

"I got the cancer," she said as I sat down across from her.

"What?" I asked, clearly taken aback by the weight of the news she had just dropped.

"Yup, I just got back from Dr. Ratzen's office. I got the cancer," she said again. "He told me it doesn't look good. I'm looking at six to eight months."

Despite the bad news, I chuckled on the inside when she said *the cancer*. My aunt is diabetic, and Grandma always referred to her condition as *the sugar*. It wasn't ha-ha funny, just one of those things.

"Where?" I finally asked, after a brief silence.

"All over," she said. She eased out of her chair, walked over to the counter, and placed a stack of windmill cookies on a plate. When she came back, she set them down on the table between us, along with two glasses of lemonade.

"How long have you had it?"

"I don't know. And it doesn't matter," she said matter-of-factly, not seeming too bothered by it. She picked up a cookie and began munching.

"The doctor said you have six to eight months?" I asked, confirming her earlier announcement.

"Yup."

We sat there in silence, waiting for the awkwardness to evaporate. This was one of those moments when I didn't know what else to say. Asking for a re-fill on my lemonade seemed inappropriate.

My grandfather had passed away three years ago. For my grandmother, it had been a very long three years. For the rest of us, our lives went back to normal, mainly because there wasn't an empty chair at our tables, but for her there was noticeable change in the way she carried herself. She wasn't miserable, but it was clear she didn't seem to enjoy things as much as she did before Grandpa died. Her focus in life seemed to have shifted. The holidays were one example. Last Christmas, the only decoration she put out was a small Christmas tree. Nothing else. When I was younger, she used to get carried away with decorations, presents, and all the other knick-knacks that accompany the holidays. Going to her house at Christmas was one of those things a boy looked forward to all year. I remember feeling disappointed when it was over. Three hundred and sixty-five more days of waiting. Watching my grandparents bring such joy to others was the best present of all. It's amazing how being in their company made me feel so content. Not the kind of content you feel when you open a present and it's exactly what you wanted. It's the kind of content that runs much deeper and lasts much longer. For the rest of your life, when you reflect on those moments, it lightens your heart and brings a smile to your face while peace permeates your entire existence.

Sitting there, I began to understand why she didn't fear death. I understood, in some small way, why she almost welcomed it. Life on this earth, for her, would soon be over, and the life she had been preparing for was soon to come. When you're separated from the one you truly love, there is a pain that only those who have experienced it can really understand. Some people know the pain that accompanies a separation for a couple of days, weeks, or even months. But the anguish that is felt when the love of your life is really gone can be compared to nothing on this earth.

I learned so much from my grandparents. What it means to serve another person well. Making an honest effort to put the needs of someone else above your own. Not having to have the last word. I watched them enrich their own lives by offering joy to others, which gave me something to think about when it came to my students at school.

Thinking about my grandparents reminded me of what Tim Fritz had told me earlier about everyone having a story. My grandma had a story, and so did my grandpa. I thought of how they had both grown up during the Great Depression. Sitting there with Grandma, I reflected on the stories she had told me when I was younger; my mind drifted to tales she would sometimes tell at family gatherings. Stories about rationing food so it would last until their family had enough money to buy more. Stories about families and neighbors coming together and growing stronger in the face of adversity, instead of looking out for their own individual needs. Stories that took on a greater meaning, now that she was getting closer to the end of her life. I was thankful for the times we had shared together. Significant memories cemented deep into my gray matter. Memories that have sunk into the marrow of my bones. I considered myself fortunate to have had the opportunity to be one of her grandchildren.

Suddenly, I was reminded of the date I had to plan with Sarah. I smiled, closed my eyes, and felt my heart lighten, hoping we could have the same kind of relationship Grandpa and Grandma had.

I love the anticipation of getting to know someone special, but for whatever reason, there was a tremendous weight around my neck regarding what to do for our date. And that's when I got my idea.

"Grandma, I'll be right back," I said to her.

"Where you going?" she asked.

"I need to check on something in the barn."

My grandpa's pole barn was like a museum of tools, instruments, and devices. Some of them dated back to the early 1900s, before he was even born.

As I walked up to the old red barn, my emotions were mixed.

My late grandfather's 1976 Chevy truck was sitting in the barn, covered with blue tarps in an effort to keep it free of bird droppings. Pulling off the tarps revealed a part of my family history. My heart lightened as I remembered Grandpa driving it in the Labor Day parade a few years before he died. As much as he loved my grandma, that truck was a close second. It's orange and cream two-tone colors were the cat's meow back in the day. As I slowly opened the driver's side door, the smell of history filled my nose. The odometer read 53,894 miles. The brown vinyl seats seemed a little dull due to the build-up of dust.

My fondest memory was when I was seven years old and my grandpa stopped by to pick me up and take me to the Taste-T-Freeze for ice cream. It was a total surprise. I kept looking over at him on the way into town. I was so proud of him. He asked me about my girlfriends, of which there were none. Seven-year-olds would do best to wait a few more years before dating. I knew he was kidding. There was such joy when I saw some of my friends from school walking on the sidewalk next to Main Street. I felt like the grand marshal of the Macy's Thanksgiving Day Parade. Grandpa honked; I waved. Despite their friendly waves, I could tell my friends were slightly jealous. Once we got there and walked up to the sliding-screen window, he said, "Get whatever you want."

"How cool is this?" I muttered to myself. *Get whatever you want.* I'd never heard that before, except from my little league coach who always added, "As long as you keep it under fifty cents." Even though the financial limits were off, I still got a single scoop of vanilla, not wanting to appear greedy. Ice cream has never tasted as good as it did that day. Sitting on the iron bench with the lime-green umbrella overhead, I knew I was having one of those moments I would never forget. His eyes sparkled as we talked. Amazing how an old truck can serve as a mental time machine.

"Grandma," I said, arriving back in the kitchen from outside, "I have a favor to ask. I was wondering if I could borrow Grandpa's truck next week."

"Oh? What's going on next week?" she asked.

"I've got a date," I said with a huge grin.

"You bet," she said in response to my question. "I'm pretty sure your grandpa would have wanted you to use it for such an extraordinary situation."

"Awesome," I said, sounding like a teenager.

"Who's the lucky young lady?"

"A girl who's been subbing in our building this year. Her name's Sarah."

"What do you have planned for this *date?*"

"I'm not really sure yet, but I thought it would be pretty cool to borrow Grandpa's truck."

I spent the rest of the evening cleaning that old Chevy. I completely forgot about eating supper. With a lot of my grandma's rags and some elbow grease, the old truck shined up pretty nice. The last time I sat behind this steering wheel, I was on my grandpa's lap. I put the keys into the ignition. Nothing. Not even a *whirrrr*. After heading in to Grandma's house to request her company, we hopped into my car and went for a ride into Hollisford, where I bought a new battery. I normally shop "local," but a lot of Coleman businesses don't stay open past the dinner hour.

Looking out the window and seeing that it was still light outside made me thankful for the transition from winter to spring. The combination of fresh spring air and longer days with more sunlight has a way of improving the overall quality of life. By the end of winter, most people in the Midwest are about ready to kill each other. The end of March, beginning of April can be a very bleak time for any Midwesterner. The bright orange and yellow maples from months ago are never enough to sustain us through winter. The most dominant colors from December through March consist of a lot of gray and brown. The winter months can sometimes drag on at a snail's pace. Seasonal Affective Disorder, caused by lack of sunlight, makes people edgy and irritable. Looks of disgust are doled out for the slightest infractions. The bottom line: people are crabby.

There was a story circulating a few years ago about an old farmer who suffered from the disorder. He gave Gretchen a tongue lashing for putting too much ice in his Coke. Unfortunately for him, she also suffers from SAD and proceeded to walk him out of the tavern by his ear lobe. Springtime is not something we take for granted.

Grandma and I made the trip and returned in record time. The new source of energy, combined with constantly shoving the gas pedal to the floor, finally caused the ol' girl to give in and decide to start. Smoke quickly filled the barn, forcing me to drive it out into the open yard. I could almost hear her sigh as she took in her first breath of fresh air in several years. It was a rough idle for a few minutes. Vehicles are a lot like us. Sit around too long, and it's hard to get moving again.

My first destination was the gas station. There's no telling how old the gas in the tank was. The old truck needed a lot of encouragement, but we managed to make it. I bought a small bottle of STP fuel treatment. Not having the time or the know-how, I was hoping this little bottle would take care of any gunk that had accumulated in the fuel lines and carburetor.

My mechanical abilities were limited to unscrewing the gas cap and changing the oil. The closest I ever came to fixing a motor was watching Thad tear into an old lawnmower given to us by one of our uncles. He did most of the work. My job was holding the old coffee can while he dropped in nuts and bolts. Even though I was of little value to him while he made his way through the carburetor, there's just something about tearing into a motor, or even just being close to someone who is, and getting some "grubby" on your hands. It gives a person a supreme feeling of satisfaction, whether you know what you're doing or not.

Thankfully, Grandpa's truck wasn't in need of any major repairs as I pulled out of the gas station. Slipping the gear lever into drive, I moved forward with the sound of crunching sand and gravel under the tires. I decided a lengthy drive would be the best way to give me the assurance that this old girl would not fail me on my date with Sarah.

After a few minutes, I came upon Bob Engal's farm, which was only a few miles from Grandma's. As a young teenager, I'd baled my fair share of hay there, earning five dollars an hour on those hot, steamy afternoons. It's funny how the harder the labor, the less money one makes.

Stopping on the side of the road, I looked out across the field, and there in the distance was the old barn where we'd stacked mountains of hay up on the second floor. I looked out across the field and smiled inside as my eyes found the spot where the field dips a little. The spot where Thad and I restacked an entire trailer of hay because we didn't do it right the first time and the bales had fallen off the trailer in one big lump, scattering as they hit the ground. My skin twitched as I recalled the chaff and dust that accumulated all over our bodies. Sometimes it took days for all the gunk to clear from our nostrils. Lugging hay bales that weighed up to seventy pounds is not for everyone. There was a sense of accomplishment as I sat there gazing out the window.

A few miles later, I stopped alongside an apple orchard, one that my family had spent considerable time in years ago. Pulling off onto the shoulder of the road, I put the truck in park, imagining the tiresome work of gathering apples. While my mom and dad were climbing ladders, filling the bushel baskets that were draped over their necks with a wide nylon strap, Thad and I would be down below on the ground, picking drops. The apples that had lost their grip and sat in the tall, wet grass under the trees were to be used to make apple cider. It was our responsibility to gather these fallen apples in a five-gallon bucket and place them in a forty-bushel crate located nearby. There was usually a small trail of battered apples on the ground running towards the huge wooden box because my little stick arms didn't quite have the girth to drag and lift a five-gallon bucket that was completely full. Rummaging through wet grass looking for apples was not something I jumped out of bed for on a Saturday morning. My young heart was full of jealousy, knowing my good buddy Clip was probably at home playing Atari video games with a bag of Fritos on the floor and a bottle of Coke serving as his after-school snack. This was hard work. Tedious. Thinking back on all those autumn afternoons somehow made me thankful for the opportunity to engage in the kind of work that made more of an impact on my character than my social life. Sitting there in the truck, I finally realized my parents didn't do this to make my life miserable; they did this to keep the bank from taking our house. And it ultimately helped me understand the importance of working hard and the lasting effects it has on a person.

I put the truck in gear and once again slowly began to move forward. There's something about time and how it tends to change our outlook. An appreciation for the way I was raised began to surface. The lean years before my mother went back to work were not fun, but they somehow shaped me into who I am. It was part of my story. My heart sank a little, thinking about my parents and how my response to them was oftentimes unfavorable. It was easy to take them for granted. While they were far from perfect, I genuinely believe they did their best in raising my brother and me. My pessimistic nature makes it easy to be critical, and the subpar attitude I sometimes held toward them was not very honoring. Feeling a little convicted of my insolence, I reached down towards the radio and pushed the pre-set station-selector button on the radio and decided I would try and do a better job of being thankful.

After tooling around the countryside and burning nearly half a tank of gas, I brought the truck back to Grandma's and parked it in the barn. I turned the motor off. It felt good to just sit and wallow in the history of that truck. Sometimes we take people for granted. We don't appreciate them as we should while they're here. I was thankful for the memories I did have of my grandfather. He wasn't a perfect man, but he was a man who made others better. He didn't do it by being preachy, just by being himself and seeing the importance of quality time with people he cared about. I was fortunate to be one those people. When the overwhelming peaceful feeling subsided, I quietly got out and shut the door, sealing in the aura that was my grandfather, and walked out to my car. Feeling very content, I might add.

"Good morning, class," I said on Monday, shortly after the first bell. "I'm glad you decided to take time out of your busy schedules to stop by for some learning." I thought a little humor might be a good way to start the week. Maybe it was just the giddiness of what lie ahead. My date with Sarah was five days away. Saturday night. No plans other than taking a joy ride in Grandpa's truck. There was definitely some anxiety, but I wasn't going to let it get in the way of my teaching. The fact that not one kid laughed or even smiled at my attempt at humor did little to discourage me. Upon further reflection, I understood why. It simply wasn't that funny. Like I mentioned earlier, if I could keep them slightly bewildered at times, not completely confused, I was better able to manage them.

While things had improved over recent months, there were still times I was reminded that I was human and I wasn't teaching in Utopia. There were still times when I would get frustrated with kids or the decisions they were making. I began to realize that I performed better in the situations for which I had practiced. I was still using my time in the car, going back and forth from home to school, to run through hypothetical situations. If a particular group of students was spending more time socializing than getting their work done, I would venture back to their area, crouch down to their level, and say, "I'm so glad everyone's getting along back here," then stop to let it sink in. "But if I have to come back here again, who should I move?" Sometimes they would point at each other, yet other times they got right back to work. I wouldn't say I *enjoyed* conflict, but when it showed up in my classroom, being prepared made all the difference.

"Today we're going to start with a new seating chart," I said. Immediately, the sound of cheers reverberated around the room. *It doesn't take much to make these kids happy,* I thought.

"Can we choose our own seats?" they all wondered. "Please? Please? Please?"

"Uhh....let me think about that for a minute," I said, trying to buy some time. This wasn't a situation I'd practiced. "Uhhhh...... sure.....why not," I mumbled looking around the room. Cheers of *hallelujah* again. It was almost as if these kids liked me.

After the shuffle of chairs and desks, we managed to proceed with the content I had planned. I was somewhat surprised, as I only had to rearrange three seats before lunch.

After walking my class to the cafeteria, I sat down at my usual seat in the teacher's lounge. While it was nice to get out of my classroom for a while, I had gotten into the habit of not staying for my entire lunch period. Two reasons mainly. The usual negative banter from some of my colleagues was one. Hearing Fran Helman say, "Boy, am I ever tired. I wish I could just go home and curl up on the couch," did nothing to improve morale. Complaining and venting have their place, just not every day during lunch. The other reason was that I enjoyed the silence of my room. The hum of fluorescent lighting can be very calming. Having some quiet time to think and reflect on the day's happenings proved to be very beneficial. Sometimes a stray thought would wander into my conscience that was actually valuable for making a positive difference in my teaching. A thought that I wouldn't have come up with if I'd been listening to staff musings.

Last week I sat in the lounge and listened to Kim Busche talk about herself for nearly twenty minutes. She was going on and on about having A.D.D. and being obsessive compulsive. Self-diagnosis, I assumed. She seemed to be rather proud of her issues and talked as though having them was a rather significant achievement. As I sat listening to her ramble on and on, I found her demeanor to be quite annoying. If I spent too much time around certain people, it was difficult to be gracious in my thoughts, so I tried to limit my time around her. Getting irritated by the likes of Kim Busche or Gus Harble proved only that I still had room to grow.

Before returning to my room, I stopped in the staff restroom. Double-checked the sign before entering, of course. I didn't want to share another private moment with a female in the bathroom like I had earlier in the year.

Before I made it back to my room, I saw a small child running down the hallway. My first reaction was to scream, "We DO NOT run in the halls!" As I had recently learned, my first response to unexpected situations wasn't always the best. After a quick second, a better idea came to mind. As the sprinting boy came closer, showing no visible sign of slowing down, I positioned myself directly into his anticipated route. When he zigzagged left, I stepped right in his path and stuck out my hand.

"Hi, I'm Mr. Carter. Who are you?" Since I had caught him off guard, he was a little stunned. I stood there shaking his hand for several seconds and asking him a variety of questions ranging from his name to whose class he was in. The last question I asked him was my favorite. Taking my sweet time, I asked, "Where do you think you'd be right now if I hadn't stopped you to ask all these silly questions?" His look of confusion only intensified as he stuck out his index finger and pointed down the hallway. Letting go of his hand, I said, "Try to remember to walk, okay?" It wasn't as exciting as screaming at him, but it was probably more effective.

During math that afternoon, things were flowing quite smoothly. Math seems to be one of the easier subjects to teach. There's not a lot of room for argument. A kid's either right or wrong. It's a pretty good return on your time, too. Spend ten to fifteen minutes showing them how to go about solving a problem, then enjoy the next half hour as they work on several problems of similar difficulty. Once in a while, I would get up to stretch my legs and walk the perimeter of the room. While I was taking my stroll, a math problem popped into my head. I counted the number of steps it took to walk around the room. Thirty-two in all. If I walked around the room eighty times, how many steps would this be? Sitting down at my desk, I scratched the problem down on a piece of notebook paper. I now had the first story problem for their multiplication test coming up at the end of the week.

Looking up from my desk, I caught a glimpse of activity out of the corner of my eye. Rob Phiss, a red-haired, glasses-wearing, pip-squeak of a kid was right in the middle of a very bad habit. He was using his index finger to pick his nose. With the butt of his hand resting gently on his chin, his finger moved like a mini-excavator, all without breaking his concentration from the multitude of math problems set before him. It was really quite amazing to watch.

Note to self: Find a new way to greet this kid in the morning. No more handshakes. Maybe an elbow-bump would suffice.

Even as I sat there watching Rob, a feeling of satisfaction came over me. I was kind of glad that I decided to stick around.

CHAPTER 12

Observation

I t was late one morning when Boggins informed me that I would be attending an in-service on reproductive health at the Central Education Offices of Northern Michigan in Traverse City on Friday. "An in-service on *what?*" I asked inquisitively.

"Reproductive health," he said again. "You know, the birds and the bees."

"You mean sex?" I asked, a little louder than necessary. His face started to turn red. His mannerisms indicated he was starting to get uncomfortable.

"Yes," he replied, walking away.

"Wait a minute," I said, following after him. "Are you sure this stuff is appropriate for sixth graders?"

"Yes, I'm sure."

"Well, how much *stuff* do I tell them?" I asked.

"Well, Ted, that's why you're going to an in-service. To find out," he said sharply. "By the way," he added, "I need to stop in your room sometime today for an observation. When's a good time?"

I mentally went through my schedule for the day. "How about right after lunch?" That's when we usually had math. Math was a pretty easy one to get through. Show a few problems, let them work quietly for a while. No sweat.

At the beginning of lunch, I found the registration form for Friday's conference was already in my mailbox. It explained that I needed to be "in-serviced" on reproductive health in order to teach it to my students. *If dogs and cats can figure this stuff out, why do I need to spend an entire day learning this material?*

I quickly realized that a substitute would be needed in my absence. *Call Sarah?* No way! The last thing I needed was to have my potential girlfriend subbing in my classroom. First of all, I couldn't take a chance on having her hear my students talk about me while I was gone. Especially if they discussed any of the negative stuff. While things had gotten better, my kids weren't exactly throwing out the welcome mat for me every morning. Apparently, some of them were holding a grudge from some of my actions earlier in the year. Secondly, what if they liked her more than me? *"Awwwww!"* they'd say when I got back. "It's you again. Why'd you have to come back?" The boys would be especially disappointed.

No, the way to go about this was to get someone who was going to make me look good. A few months ago when Harble was sick, he had this extremely ancient substitute who screamed and yelled all day. Not much different than Harble himself, but with the adjustments and improvements I had recently made, this lady was sure to make me look first-rate.

"What was the name of that sub you had a while back when you were sick?" I asked Gus during lunch in the lounge.

"I don't know; why?" he asked. "You thinking about asking her out?" He started to laugh. I, however, didn't find his brand of humor very funny.

"Yeah," I said sarcastically. "I'm looking to hook up with someone about the same age as my great-grandmother. Hopefully things will work out so we can get married, I'll take out a huge life-insurance policy, then, if I'm lucky, she'll die, and I won't have to work with knuckle-heads like you anymore."

Whooops! He just stood there for a second, not believing what I had just said. For way too long, this guy had been a burr under my saddle. It would feel good to start paying him back a little bit. The old Ted was still in there somewhere, trying to bust out during these moments of weakness. The old Ted would have been way too thrilled to give this guy a huge dose of his own medicine, and while it was very difficult at times, the new Ted was going to try and be a little more gracious. True, my sarcastic response was not very polite, but no one's perfect.

I got the sub's name and number from Carol in the office. "That was Sally Ankerschmidt," she told me. She paused a moment and then asked me why I wanted her to sub for me. "How about that cute girl who was here for Helen?" she asked, referring to Sarah. "The one you're always talking to when she's here."

"Oh, I guess I didn't think about her," I said, laughing.

"And why do you want that lady who was here for Gus?" she asked. "I don't think she was very good with the kids."

"Uh...are you sure?" I asked. "Those kids seemed to be falling right in line. She looks like someone with good classroom management."

"She just seemed kind of crabby," said Carol. "Like she didn't really want to be here."

You wouldn't want to be here either, I thought to myself, *if you were closing in on a hundred and spent your last days as a substitute teacher.*

"Thanks, Carol."

Then she asked, "Where are you going anyway? Are you taking a vacation day?"

"No," I said with a grimace. "I'm going to an in-service to learn about the birds and the bees."

"Oh," she said. "Have fun. Hope you learn something."

The end of my week was going to be full of action. In-service on Friday. Date on Saturday.

Lunchtime evaporated rather quickly, and it was time to get back to my room. I wasn't even nervous until Boggins showed up right before the lunch period ended, meaning the kids would be coming in loud, and I'd have to try and get them settled while he was there in the room. I was hoping that he'd come a little later, in case I had to raise my voice to get them settled down.

His early arrival wasn't my first surprise of the day. When I woke up this morning, there was some tightness around the outer edge of my nose. It was a tightness that was very painful to the touch. Further investigation revealed a zit forming in the fold where my nose and cheek met. If history was any indicator, this baby was going to be in full bloom by Saturday, complete with its own pulse. *Great,* I thought. Just in time for date night. Sarah would be so mesmerized by my pimple that she wouldn't listen to a word I was saying. *Just relax,* I told myself, and most importantly—*Don't touch it!*

As Boggins sat down at the back of the room, my nerves started to get the better of me. I panicked. On the outside I was trying to give off the calm, cool, and collected vibe, but on the inside my guts were loosening, trying to decide if my lunch was going to return by the same route it had entered or find another way to exit my body.

Just for fun, and to try and relax my nerves a little, I said in a rather unusual way, "Okay, class, let's settle down. Simmer." Waiting exactly two seconds, I said, "Simmer," one more time, just like Ms. Horter used to do. Boggins looked up from his notepad and shook his head. My class was a little surprised, too, allowing me a chance to tell them to sit down and get their math books out.

I forgot to tell my class that Boggins was coming in the afternoon. "Why's Mr. Boggins here?" Bryan Brookens yelled from the corner of the room.

"Mr. Boggins is here, class," I said slowly, "because he wants to get a sense of what's happening in here." Regret for not having told them earlier hit me hard. It would have been nice to warn them and say something like, "All right, listen up, everyone. Mr. Boggins is stopping by after lunch to observe me teach math. You need to know he's going to be watching you too. If you talk out of turn, daydream, or do something to draw unnecessary attention to yourself, he's going to put you in detention for the remainder of the month." However, with him in the room, I had to keep it short and to the point, and most importantly, tell the truth. "Mr. Boggins will be sitting in on our math lesson today, kids. So let's do everything we can to make him feel comfortable."

As I began the lesson, the kids were hanging in there pretty well. Most of them were paying attention, which is really all one can hope for after lunch. Boggins was at the back, scribbling away on his notepad. *What on earth could he be writing about back there?* I wondered.

It was extremely nerve-wracking to have him in my room while I was trying to teach. I managed to do a decent job; however, halfway through the lesson I remembered that I should probably walk around the room a little more than I usually do to improve my image. I had enough sense to know that plopping down at my desk wasn't going to put me in the best light. Some of the kids were exchanging puzzled looks as I perused the aisles more often than normal. They're not dummies. They knew what I was doing.

After a half hour, he left. Watching him walk out the door allowed my entire body to relax. It was like taking off a sixty-pound backpack.

The rest of the day went by without any major hiccups. After school, I racked my brains for almost two hours trying to come up with sub plans for Friday. Even though the in-service was a few days away, I didn't want to wait until the last minute. When I finally finished, there were almost three pages of notes. These plans were so detailed, a monkey could teach this class—assuming he was able to read.

On my way out of school, I stopped by my mailbox one last time. I found a write-up on school stationary in my mailbox. It said: *Great job, Ted! Looks like those kids really enjoy math. Keep up the good work.* I don't know what he did with all the notes he had taken during my observation, but the three sentences he'd left in my mailbox were all the encouragement I needed. Thank goodness he hadn't observed me at the beginning of the year. Leaving the workroom, I saw the same school stationary in Kim Busche's mailbox. Her box was right below mine. *Should I?* Her note from Boggins was really none of my business. For a brief second, I struggled with doing the right thing, and then I slowly headed for the door. *Aw, what the heck.* I ambled back to my mailbox, pretending that I'd forgotten something. Feeling around the empty space that was my mailbox, I glanced down at the contents in hers. It read: *Great work, Kim! It looks like those kids really like science. Keep up the good work.*

Driving to Traverse City on Friday morning gave me some good "windshield time." That was a term coined by a college friend in reference to a long trip with several hours in a car by oneself. My pores were starting to percolate with the anticipation of tomorrow night's activities. My mind wandered off to another time I had a first date during my freshman year of college. There were a couple of things I took from the experience. Make sure to bring your wallet. It was a little embarrassing asking my date for a short-term loan. While that wasn't a deal breaker, I also learned to double-check the business hours of the place you were planning to visit. Waiting forty-five minutes for the bowling alley to open was not a good move. Combined with the fact that there was no love connection, the first date was also our last.

I also thought about the times when my stomach would get so wigged out by the excitement and nervousness of a first date that it would make all kinds of weird gurgling noises, like the sound of gigantic steel beams being bent and twisted out of shape.

After parking my car in the huge parking lot of the Central Education Office, I briskly walked into the building, following a herd of people through two gigantic glass double doors. Walking into the large room, complete with dozens of round tables, I felt like I was in high school again, trying to find a place to sit down. Walking around, trying to look confident, but not knowing anyone, made it awkward to find a seat. Most of us in the room were first-year teachers. There were a few older ones scattered around. There were even a few familiar faces. Acquaintances from college. I didn't bother to talk to anyone, as they were just people I shared a few classes with, nothing more. Since I'm not into small talk, I just kept my greeting to a half-smile and a quick downward nod of my head. That was enough.

The presenter proceeded to do one of the most amazing magic tricks I've ever seen. She took fifteen minutes of information and stretched it into six hours of facts and data. By the end of the day, I was more exhausted than if I had been teaching. Sitting, listening to someone drone on and on, has a way of draining the energy from a person. It was a little discouraging, too, since I hadn't really learned anything. I had an "A-ha" moment when she explained that since most parents don't take time to discuss this stuff with their kids, it was up to the schools to take care of it. I smiled and shook my head, thinking of my dad and his not having "filled-me-in" when I was younger. It was my mom who ended up sitting my brother and me down on the couch one Saturday afternoon, making us read a book called *How Babies are Made*. Talk about awkward.

I awoke Saturday morning to bright sunshine beaming through my bedroom window. It felt good to sleep in. The clock read a little after nine o'clock. Normally at this time on a weekday, I'd be in teaching mode. Rolling out of bed, I pulled on some sweatpants. The same gray ones I'd been wearing since high school.

"Mornin', Mom," I said pouring myself a cup of coffee. My dad was sitting down at the table, probably on his third or fourth cup by now. I started to get tense, knowing what I needed to do. Before I could talk myself out of it, I said, "Mom…Dad… I want to apologize for taking you two for granted. I appreciate you two letting me live here, and I know I haven't done a very good job of being thankful. So, I just wanted to say 'thanks' for everything."

They both looked at me like I was talking in Spanish. When I practiced in my head, it looked and sounded different. They were supposed to say, "Hey, we know living with your parents at your age can create some problems, but we understand. Don't worry about it, son." Instead, my dad continued to look at me like I was speaking a foreign language, and my mom simply said, "Sure." Hmmm. Oh well, I couldn't control their response. Taking care of my end of things made me feel better, even though it caused a brief moment of uneasiness.

To help make the afternoon go a little faster, I decided on an unannounced visit with Tim Fritz. I was relieved to see that he was home. The sound of crunching gravel as I pulled into his driveway must have alerted him that somebody had arrived. He opened his front door and came out of the house with a huge smile on his face. "I was wondering when I'd see you again," he said with genuine enthusiasm.

"Well, I figured I'd stop by and see how you were doing," I said, laughing.

We didn't talk about anything in particular. It was nice to enjoy some good conversation and take my mind away from the nervousness that first dates seem to evoke.

He offered me a late lunch, and I was happy to accept. After thanking him for the visit, I slowly made my way home.

An hour before I was to leave to pick up Sarah, I hopped in the shower and after doing the normal things, I continued to stand in the hot water. Looking toward the corner of the tub, my razor sat there tempting me. "Not this time," I said out loud, referring to the hack-job I did on my upper lip on the first day of school. I'd rather have stubble on my chin than a gross scab on my face. Maybe it was the hot water, or maybe it was just pure luck, but feeling around my face, I found that the zit had diminished. *Hallelujah!!!*

Stepping out of the shower, I studied myself intently. Tilting my head down, I could see an area on the crown of my head that had a little more scalp showing than a year ago. To make myself feel better, I turned sideways to look at my profile. "I've still got it," I said out loud, referring to my chest and shoulders. Taking my right arm, I curled it up and made a fist. The ol' biceps were still there too. I turned to face the mirror again, looking at myself straight on, with both arms flexing, curled in the direction of my head. My clenched fists only inches from my ears. Leaning my head toward my right bicep, I pursed my lips and gave it a little kiss. Before leaning in the other direction to kiss my left bicep, I stopped, gave myself a wink and a nod. It was at this exact moment, my dad opened the door.

"What are you doing?" he asked.

"Just getting ready to go out," I replied, slightly embarrassed. He stood there staring at me like he had earlier that morning. Before he receded back into the hallway, I said, "Dad, if it's not too much to ask, could you please knock on the door when you see that it's closed?"

"I'll try," his muffled voice came from the other side of the door.

"Thanks," I muttered to myself.

After putting a few extra strokes of deodorant under my armpits, it was time to get dressed and be on my way.

CHAPTER 13

A Night to Remember

I had to admit, it seemed weird. I never imagined I'd be going out with a girl from Hollisford. It was like that episode on *The Dukes of Hazzard* when Daisy got engaged to Boss Hog's nephew. Things like this just weren't supposed to happen.

After pulling into the driveway and taking a deep breath, I casually slid out of the seat and closed the door. It didn't shut completely, so I had to open it up and slam it shut. Checking to make sure everything was tucked in and zipped up, I approached the door, gave it a hearty knock-knock, and waited in silence. Finally, the sound of heavy footsteps could be heard approaching. I was hoping her mother would answer, but judging by the heavy thuds coming from the other side of the door, it was more than likely not.

"Hello," her dad said as he opened the door. "Come on in."

He looked nothing like what I expected. Visions of a handsome, glasses-wearing older man dressed in a sport coat with a pipe in one hand and a copy of *War and Peace* in the other is not what I saw. Instead, a burly, middle-aged man wearing blue jeans and a Michigan State sweatshirt watched intently as I walked through the entryway into the kitchen.

"I'm Mike Buzkernski," he said, reaching out to shake my hand. His mammoth claw swallowed mine.

"Hi. I'm Ted Carter," I said while giving him two firm pumps.

"Come on in. Have a seat," he said walking towards the living room. "I've got a few questions for you."

"So you're from Coleman?" he wondered out loud after he sat down in his recliner. I managed to sit right in the middle of the couch, facing him. "You don't happen to know the Deeters off Highway Two, do you?"

"Well, I know who they are," I replied. "One of their kids graduated with my brother."

"I work with Tom Deeters." He sat there looking at me for a second. He wasn't glaring at me or anything, more than likely he was deciding what question to ask next. He was probably trying to find out if he knew anyone who knew me. As soon as we left, he'd probably be on the phone calling that person to see just exactly who his daughter would be out with tonight.

"Got big plans tonight?" he asked.

"No, sir," I said. "We're just going to have some dinner, and I'll be sure to have her home at a reasonable time."

Judging by the look on his face, it was hard to tell if this guy was for real. He was either very protective of his daughter, or he was getting some sort of pleasure making me feel uncomfortable. Whatever the case, at that moment, I decided if I were ever blessed with a daughter, her boyfriend was going to go through the same thing.

"Hello," came that angelic voice that sent my insides wobbling.

"So, where are you two going tonight?" her mother asked, following her into the living room.

Up until two hours before picking her up, I honestly had no idea where we were going. Rusty's Roadhouse was definitely out of the equation. I realize most dreams don't come true, but why take chances? I had picked a place certain to give us privacy like no other spot.

Not wanting to come off as a creep, I lied to her mother. "We're going to head to Rusty's," I said as confidently as I could. I shot a quick look at Sarah. She didn't seem to be repulsed by the idea. The reason I lied was because I wanted to surprise her, and I didn't think her parents would appreciate a stranger saying something along the lines of "It's a secret. I can't tell you." My insides felt a little weird having just lied, but it was a risk I was willing to take.

"What year's that truck?" her father asked, pointing out towards the driveway.

"It's a '76," I told him.

He said, "I used to have a '77." His eyes drifted back like he was remembering a favorite memory from his yesteryears. "Never should've got rid that thing," he said regretfully. "That got a three-fifty in it?"

"Um...yeah...I think it does. It used to be my grandpa's until he passed away."

"Those engines will go forever if you treat 'em right," he said. "Had almost two-hundred thousand on mine." Pausing for a moment, he continued. "That the original paint?"

"I believe so," I said.

We stood inside for a few more minutes. As we walked out the front door and out to the truck, it seemed like her dad was putting himself in position to go with us. He walked up to the truck and ran his hand along the box, scrutinizing the truck more than he had me.

"You better take care of this old girl," he went on. For a second, I thought he was talking about Sarah. "You don't see too many trucks like this on the road anymore."

"Not unless they're spotted with rust," I said confidently. It was like the truck had magically bridged the gap between her father and me. I can't be sure, but I figure if the father of the girl you're taking out likes your truck, you're off to a good start.

I had almost forgotten to open the door for Sarah. Walking over to my side of the truck for a split second, I remembered my manners and quickly jogged over to her side, opened the door, and shut it once all her body parts cleared the threshold.

Making my way to the other side, I glanced at her parents. I smiled. They smiled. I almost pinched myself to make sure I wasn't dreaming this time. Hopping up in the seat, I put on my seatbelt, turned the key in the ignition, and soon we were on our way.

"So is Rusty's where you take all your dates?" she asked with a smile.

"Well, actually...we're not going to Rusty's," I told her.

"Oh," she said quietly.

Not waiting for the silence to grow too large, I responded, "I know this out-of-the-way place, but I wanted to keep it a secret." It didn't sound as profound out loud as it had in my mind. "I wish I could tell you, but then it wouldn't be a surprise," I said with a mysterious grin.

We rode on toward our destination. At times there was a quiet silence. Definitely not awkward. My pits were cooperating, which is always a good sign. It was hard to put words to how I was feeling at that moment, but *comfortable* comes to mind. There was something so genuine, so real about this girl. There wasn't any temptation to try and impress her with half-truths or even flat out lies. We chattered back and forth in an easy, carefree sort of way as we cruised the roads in my grandpa's Chevy. Having remembered the first time I saw her earlier in the year, I asked, "So...what were you doing at Gretchen's a while ago?"

"Who's Gretchen?" she asked.

"Gretchen's Irish Pub. That place where I first saw you. You came in and talked to the owner, that short lady. I was sitting off to the side, watching you..." I stopped right there for a second. "Watching you eat," I said rather sheepishly.

"That was you!?" she exclaimed. "The guy who kept staring at me, but every time I looked over in your direction, you put your head down. That was you?"

"Uh...yes, that was me. What was a nice girl like you doing in Coleman, eating at Gretchen's?" I asked in a joking manner, though there was a tinge of seriousness in my voice.

"What do you mean what was a *nice* girl like me doing in Coleman?"

"You know," I went on, quickly realizing I was about to dig

myself into a hole, "I was just surprised to see someone like you in Coleman."

"Someone like me?" she asked quizzically. "What are you talking about?"

"You know...the chances of a guy from Coleman and a girl from Hollisford are...well, you know...pretty slim."

"Haven't you ever read *The Outsiders*?" she asked, referring to S.E. Hinton's book, written in the late 1960s, which dealt with the struggles between the *haves* and the *have-nots*.

Averting my gaze from the road for a quick second, I looked across the cab of the truck and gave her a half grin, understanding the theme to which she was referring. "Yeah, I think I read it in eighth grade."

"Maybe you need to read it again," she said with a laugh.

Getting back to my question, she continued, "I was stopping in to grab a bite to eat. That lady, Gretchen, was telling me where the school was, because I was planning to substitute teach, and I didn't remember exactly how to get there. I had been there a few times in high school to watch some friends play basketball, but I'm directionally challenged, somewhat."

I went on to tell her how I had worked there on and off through college.

Pulling into my grandma's driveway caused me to smile just a bit too broadly.

"Who lives here?" she asked.

"My grandma."

"Are we here to pick something up?" she asked.

"No, we're here to eat."

"Does she know you're coming?"

"You don't think I'd drop by my grandma's house for dinner without giving her a heads up, do ya?"

The nervousness that had sloshed in my gut for so many weeks faded like the Midwest winter sun. While I had been unsure of the response I'd get over my choice of location for dinner, her nonchalant manner of getting out of the truck and walking up the front steps, like this was no big deal, sent invisible signals through the air.

They screamed, *I'm all right with this!!!* As I opened the front door, it was refreshing to see a huge smile spread across her face. Sure, this wasn't like renting an airplane and flying her to Chicago for dinner, but something about the way she walked into the kitchen let me know I was on the verge of something special.

There in the middle of the kitchen was a collection of matching bowls and plates already set on the table. The bowls were filled with fresh lettuce, cucumbers, and carrots. In the middle of the table, a loaf of homemade bread, still steaming, sat on the cutting board. The smell of fresh percolated coffee swirled and mixed in with the other smells. Over by the stove, my grandma was keeping an eye on the spaghetti sauce.

Earlier in the day, I had finally made up my mind. Having dinner at my grandma's house would allow me to accomplish what I wanted—doing something out of the ordinary and avoiding a noisy, crowded restaurant with the possibility of seeing one of my students.

"Hello, Sarah," my grandma said, turning around to face us. The front of her apron was splattered red with tomato sauce, making her look more like a serial killer than my grandmother.

Without the slightest bit of hesitation, the two of them met in the middle of the kitchen for a quick hug, like they had known each other for years.

"It's so nice to meet you," Sarah said, backing away from the embrace.

"You two are just in time," said Grandma, turning back to the stove. "Dinner will be ready in about two minutes." She quickly added, "Ted, would you please light the candles?"

It was sort of strange. I was expecting things to be a little bit uncomfortable, since I'd never heard of anyone taking his girlfriend to his elderly grandparent's house on a date. Let alone a first date.

Sitting down at the table, the wonderful smells combined with the soft glow of the candles allowed this moment to etch deep into my brain. After asking the blessing, we commenced to eating. Doing my best to chew slowly and wait until my mouth was empty before engaging in conversation took every ounce of self-control. I knew spaghetti was a safe bet. Sure, there was the probability a guy could drip sauce down the front of his shirt, but that was better than taking a chance on tearing into a piece of grisly steak or chicken, only to end up trying to discreetly spit it into a napkin. It's difficult to do that gracefully, so I went with something that could be more easily chewed.

Using my best manners, I managed to make it through the whole meal without any mishaps. After almost every bite, I wiped my napkin across my mouth to reduce the chances of my supper getting stuck on my face. By the end of the meal, my lips were a bit raw from all the wiping. My napkin, which at the beginning of the meal was white but was now a faint orange, lay wadded up into a little ball on my lap.

After dinner, Sarah and I went into the living room. In the corner of the room on a small table sat the checkerboard and checkers my grandpa and I played when I was little. It hadn't been used much lately. "You know anything about checkers?" I asked Sarah as she looked for a place to sit.

"I sure do," she replied. "Is that a challenge?" We both walked to the corner. I slid the table out away from the wall. Grabbing the ottoman, I slid it over to one side of the table.

"Here you are, my..." I stuttered. I almost said, "Here you are, my dear," but stopped just in time. Our relationship wasn't quite ready for that. My face warmed a little. By the look on her face, it was clear she was aware what I had almost said.

The checker game was a good way to avoid forced conversation. Taking turns, it was clear she was not a novice.

We could hear my grandma doing dishes in the kitchen. Looking away from the game, I watched her for a minute as she washed and rinsed. When I was barely able to walk, I used to pull a chair up beside her and help her wash dishes. I would take a bowl or a spoon and dip it into the soapy water, moving it to and fro. In hindsight, helping her probably caused the process to take longer, but she never seemed to mind. Some of my favorite memories happened in her kitchen. Every summer she canned peaches, and I was always her little helper. My favorite part was eating the long strings of peach peels she cut off with her wooden-handled paring knife. She'd throw a section of peach skin my way every once in a while with just the slightest flick of her wrist.

The clatter of plates and silverware could be heard as she put them into the dish drainer. For a brief moment, my mind went back to the days when I would watch my grandpa help her with the dishes. It wasn't something I ever saw him do by himself, but apparently his love for his wife was strong enough that he would use any excuse possible to be near her. I could almost hear him laughing. Despite the optimistic vibe I felt, being on an actual date with an actual girl, there was a tinge of melancholy as I watched my grandma rinse the last dish.

"Are you going to move?" Sarah asked, breaking the silence.

"Huh?"

"It's your turn," she said.

"Oh, right." As I studied the board, it was clear that I was about to get whooped. Which, in turn, made me wonder how long I had been daydreaming. Perhaps she had made more than one move; how would I know? Looking up from the board, looking into Sarah's eyes, my heart swelled. Smiling, I looked back at the board, moved my red checker to just the right spot. The spot that allowed her to take my remaining three checkers. "Good game," I said, laughing.

"I get winner," Grandma said as she walked into the room.

"That would *not* be me," I said, making light of my checker skills. Or lack thereof.

Watching my girlfriend and my grandma play checkers was almost surreal.

We ended up staying for quite a while, but as much fun as we were having, it was getting late. "It was nice meeting you, Sarah," Grandma said as we both knelt down to tie our shoes on the way out.

"It was nice meeting you too," Sarah said.

We exchanged hugs with Grandma and walked outside. The tension was building as we got back in the truck. I knew the idea of a "first kiss" when I dropped her off at home was more than likely racing through her mind as well.

Taking a deep breath, I decided to put out some feelers. "So, where do you see this thing going?" I asked. The words hung in the space between us. My skin prickled in anticipation of what she might say. The brief stillness in verbal activity caused me to panic a little, and my right armpit tightened.

And then, after giving it enough time to sink in and prepare a response, she said, "If you think I'm falling for that, you're crazy. I know how guys work. If you think I'm going to be the first one to say how I feel about us, you've got another thing coming." Looking over I could see her smile, giving me all the information I needed.

"So what are you doing next Saturday?" I asked with feigned macho-ism.

"I don't know. That's a long way off," she replied. "I like to take things one day at a time." It was quiet for a moment, and then slowly, she unbuckled her seatbelt and slid over to the middle of the big bench seat right next to me. Reaching over with her left hand, she grabbed my right hand from the steering wheel and proceeded to drape my arm over her shoulder. "Hopefully, you'll call me before then," she said.

"I don't think that will be a problem," I assured her. "That will definitely not be a problem."

Seeing as I was in no hurry to take her home, it made perfect sense to put a few miles on the Chevy. Because it was a three-quarter ton truck and designed for heavy loads, it rode like an army tank. Even the slightest bump in the road made us bounce and jiggle. The friction caused by our shoulders rubbing together, combined with a hint of her perfume, caused my heart to shoot off fireworks. "Why are you driving so slow?" she wondered aloud.

Looking down at the speedometer, it was bouncing in quick rhythmic gyrations in front of the thirty-five. Rather bravely, I replied, "I guess I'm in no hurry for this night to be over." At this point I was really quite impressed by my confidence, though I didn't want to get too carried away and say something really corny. My brain kept throwing out things to say. Fortunately, there was enough of a delay between my brain and mouth that most of it went unsaid. After another moment of just listening to the tires hum, I asked, "You wouldn't happen to be in the mood for ice cream?"

"I was hoping you weren't going to take me home just yet. Ice cream sounds wonderful."

We continued on until we came to the Taste-T-Freeze. There was a decent line of people waiting for sundaes and ice cream cones. Even Harold, the owner, was helping tonight. Pulling into a vacant spot, I shut off the engine. Neither one of us moved. Our hands were still touching. I looked in the direction of the lines of people shuffling towards the window ledge. Because it was spring, most of the people in line were out simply celebrating the fact that they weren't stuck inside. Being cooped up inside for six months during the winter makes something as simple as going to the Taste-T-Freeze and paying three times as much for ice cream seem like a good idea.

"See that table over there?" I said to Sarah, pointing off to the right. "That's where my grandpa and I always sat."

She looked up at me and smiled. And for a nanosecond it entered my mind to kiss her. Right on the lips. Then it passed. We sat there a while longer, waiting for the lines of people to dissipate.

Eventually, we got out and walked towards the counter. "Get whatever you want," I said. "No limit tonight." The grin on my face was a dead giveaway that I was just fooling around.

Without missing a beat, she said, "Thanks, coach."

After getting our orders, we strolled down the beat up sidewalk toward the picnic tables. I put my hand on her arm as we came to the spot where the sidewalk suddenly jutted upward like a miniscule version of plate tectonics. I knew if she tripped and dropped her cone, Harold wasn't going to give her another one unless I paid for it. Besides, it also gave me a reason to touch her arm. "Careful now," I told her. "There've been a lot of disappointed people in this spot right here. I think the reason Harold hasn't fixed the sidewalk is because this little bump gives him a lot of extra business." We walked over and sat down.

"If I happen to smear ice cream across my face, do me a favor and don't tell me, okay," I told her in a preemptive way to lighten the mood, just in case I did get some ice cream on my face. Even though I was feeling confident, I didn't want something like a messy face to get in the way.

"Sure thing," she said as she sat down.

It was one of those late spring evenings people dream about. The sun was setting, and an orange glow seemed to vibrate in the western sky. Silhouettes of houses and trees stood like giant shadows against the flaming sky. It was just cool enough that in order to stay warm, we needed to sit right next to each other, leaving barely enough room to slide a piece of notebook paper the skinny way between us. Overhead, stars were beginning to dot the heavens. New ones appeared every few minutes.

At some point during our conversation and the consumption of my ice cream, it became clear to me that Sarah and I were on the brink of something grand and glorious. Looking up towards the heavens, I managed to express my thankfulness for this moment... without saying a single word.

CHAPTER 14

Contentment

With my date with Sarah ending the way I hoped, there was an optimism pulsating through my body. Driving home felt good. It was quite pleasant not worrying whether or not she wanted to go out again.

By the time I slipped into bed, the clock read 12:58 a.m., and it was another hour before my senses calmed down enough for my body to drift off.

Despite the late night, I still woke up early enough to get ready for church. Somewhere between taking a shower and finding clean clothes, I tried calling my grandma to see if she was still planning on having me pick her up. The phone rang and rang. It seemed strange hearing her answering machine come on. I didn't even know she had one. "Hey, grandma…it's Ted. Just calling to see if you were still…" My voice trailed off. For some strange reason, my heart began to speed up, and my hands got all clammy. The thought of my grandmother's lifeless body lying in bed flashed through my brain. Quickly ending the call, I re-dialed her number. It rang several times again before the answering machine picked up once more. "Hello, you've reached…." Her voice faded away as I slammed the phone down.

Racing out to the truck, I got in, slammed the door, and sped over to Grandma's house. Pulling into the driveway, I rushed out of the truck and sprinted for her front door. One attempt at turning the doorknob revealed it was locked. Her house seemed still and lifeless. Looking through the front door, her house was completely quiet. "Sweet Mother of Moses," I said. Running around behind the house, I found the spare key she kept in a magnetic key holder inside the metal pipes my grandfather welded together to make poles for a clothesline. Running back to the front door, I forced the key in the lock and shoved the door open. "Grandma! Grandma!" I yelled. Running through the house, I went straight for her bedroom. Seeing that the door to her room was shut, I stopped. My knees went weak, and my stomach lurched up into my throat. Not having the strength to open the door and face reality, I put my head down.

"What on earth are you doing !?!" a familiar voice yelled from down the hall in the direction of the living room.

"What?" I said, suddenly turning in the direction of my grandma's voice.

"What on earth are you doing?" she asked again.

Staring in disbelief, I started to say, "I thought you were…" but I couldn't bring myself to say it.

"Dead?" she asked over raised eyebrows.

"Why didn't you answer your phone?" I asked. "I was calling to make sure you were still planning on having me pick you up."

"Oh, was that you? I must have fallen asleep on the sofa waiting for you. I thought I heard the phone ring. You and your girlfriend had me up pretty late last night," she said through smiling eyes. "I'm not a spring chicken anymore."

We loaded up into the old Chevy and made our way into town. It was fun driving this truck. The old memories intertwined with new ones.

After church, I dropped her back off at home. "Grandma," I said, "please don't scare me like that again."

"I'll try not to," she said, laughing. She slammed the door closed. Not because she was angry or anything; that's just the way these old doors had to be shut.

"See you later," I called out through the half-open window.

"Oh, wait a minute," she called. "There's something I wanted to tell you."

Pushing down on the brake, I put the gear shifter back in park. "What's that?" I asked.

"I think your grandpa would have wanted you to keep this truck," she told me. "It doesn't do anyone any good sitting in the barn."

"Thanks, Grandma," I told her.

"You're welcome," she said with a wink. "Enjoy the rest of your day," she told me before I left.

Instead of turning in the direction of home, I took a left turn towards Hollisford. It crossed my mind to see if there was anyone interested in a Sunday drive.

As the end of the school year got closer and closer, the weeks flew by. Early one Friday morning, Carol's voice boomed over the intercom.

"Attention, teachers," she said, "please meet in the teacher's workroom for a quick meeting with Mr. Boggins."

Getting up from my desk, I strolled out of my room and down the hallway.

I entered the workroom and noticed Boggins was holding a pile of papers in his hand. As the last of my colleagues filtered in, he began, "The MEAT results are in, and I have some good news." He paused for dramatic effect. "Our scores have improved almost five points overall."

There were some "oohs" and "aahs" from a few of the teachers. Not really understanding the significance of five points, I kept quiet.

It was obvious he was proud, though I knew better than to get overly excited about these tests. Even though this was only my first year of teaching, I knew that one test, on one particular day, doesn't measure all that a person knows or has accomplished.   It made me feel bad for Boggins. Here he was, acting like a kid on Christmas morning, almost as if he believed he had something to do with the improvement. I chuckled to myself. This is not where real life lies. Real life doesn't lie in some standardized test score. Real life lies in the day-to-day happenings. Those unscripted moments when you come up with something cool and clever, and there's no one in your classroom except you and your students. Those moments that leave you feeling content, almost as though you were called to be a teacher. Thinking about how much I'd grown this year, it was clear there wasn't a test I could take to show people the areas in which I'd improved. There wasn't any test I could take to show that I understood the importance of everyone's story and how there's a lot more to a person than meets the eye. There wasn't a test to prove that I had a better understanding of the importance of being gracious to others. There's no test for these areas of our lives, but if you're fortunate enough to realize these things, you just keep it to yourself and hope you have an opportunity down the line to share it with others. That's what really matters, not a test score, which only seems to excite the ones wearing suits and ties.

Truth be told, I know I learned more than the kids in my class, though I wouldn't go around bragging about it. Who would I tell, anyway?

After rambling on for a few minutes, he concluded by saying, "Keep up the good work, everyone." As was usually the case, people started making their way toward the exit before he finished talking.

Today was the day I was to present the "facts of life" to the boys in my class. The girls were going to be watching a video called *What it Means to be a Woman* with Carol in a little room next to the office. As the girls filed out, leaving me with the boys, the tension in the room began to tighten. My armpits were warming up. I put two t-shirts on underneath my dress shirt this morning, knowing it would take a while for the perspiration to make its way through three layers of clothing.

Trying to stall as much as I could, I told them to grab a pencil and some notebook paper, but instead of saying pencil, I said another word with the same beginning sound—the very part of their bodies that kept them in here with me. Howls of laughter erupted like Mt. St. Helens. Waiting a second for it to subside, I continued talking over their giggles. "And some notebook paper before you bring your chairs up front," I said, revealing some anxiety. The old Ted would have yelled something like, "EXCUSE ME!!!! This is not funny." But deep down it was kind of funny, so I joined in the laughter. After it died down, I began my presentation.

At that moment, I decided to be spontaneous and try and have some fun with these guys. "Boys," I said. "You know why we're here. To get us started, we're going to review a few things." My goal was to put them at ease. Starting with the basics, I went on to explain where and how most of the changes would occur and when they were likely to happen.

Talking about male anatomy always seems to bring on the giggles. It was impossible to keep the corners of my mouth from turning up, too, when certain words were said. I'm not sure how much they actually learned.

I had planned to spend ten or fifteen minutes talking about the changes they either had been experiencing or were about to encounter. In my nervousness, it took about two. Fortunately, the district provided a fifteen minute video called *Becoming a Man* that discussed in greater detail some of the topics I had quickly gone over. Every time the video mentioned a certain word, they all laughed, including me.

At the conclusion of the video, I had each kid write down a question they had or something they learned about this topic. "You have to write something down," I demanded. "All the pencils need to be moving." They took a minute to write something down. "This is going to sound a little strange, guys, but DO NOT put your name on your paper." I gathered their papers; there was some nervous chatter as they waited for me to sift through them.

Standing in front, I began to read through the papers. The first one read, "When will I get hair?" As I went on to explain that everybody is different and that changes happen at different times, I saw some heads nodding. Some of them looked relieved. A lot of their questions were the same, making it clear many of them were wondering the same things. Towards the bottom of the pile, one read, "Why is your face so red?" I decided to leave that one alone.

One thing I had learned this year was the importance of timing. That's why this little talk was scheduled for the very end of the day. As soon as I finished, they were dismissed. They were free to leave. Watching them walk out of the room, it was clear to me that they were ready for this talk. A lot of them were wearing pants that stopped about two inches above their ankles. Shortly after they left, I headed home too.

Even though things went well, I was totally exhausted at the end of the day. Talking about puberty with adolescent boys took some juice from my battery.

I was still a bit amped up on the way home and noticed that I still had a good sweat going. The back of my shirt was sticking like Velcro to the seat.

There was another thing I was beginning to realize, too. Regardless of whether it had been a good week or a bad week, Friday afternoon always felt good.

The end of the year was right around the corner. One week to go. Recently, on the way home, I heard a DJ mention that the weather was supposed to heat up to unseasonably warm temperatures. As if the kids weren't squirrely enough, the hot weather was only going to add to the craziness.

The last week of school was a blur. To be honest, there wasn't a lot of learning being done. And to be even more honest, there wasn't a lot of teaching going on either. Mostly, I did my best to keep them busy. We had a checkers tournament that took most of an entire day. There were several games of mumball, which involved them throwing a ball back and forth without talking. (Too bad I hadn't thought to play this earlier in the year.) I even showed them how to play euchre with moderate success. On the last day of school, we walked downtown to Comet Lanes for some bowling. I even allowed enough time to stop by the Taste-T-Freeze. "Get whatever you want," I told them. My announcement was met with cheers and shrieks of excitement. Then, like my old baseball coach, I said, "As long as you keep it under fifty cents."

It was quickly brought to my attention that there wasn't anything on the list of options for fifty cents. Thankfully, I'd had enough sense to call Harold ahead of time to let him know we were stopping by. He already had small bowls of soft-serve ice cream served up. The only thing my students needed to tell him was whether they wanted chocolate syrup or strawberry and whether or not they wanted nuts.

"You're the best teacher ever," Ann Rosenthal told me as we made our way back to school. I secretly wondered if she would have said that had I not bought her an ice cream sundae. Probably not. I was thankful for the compliment, especially since I had made her cry earlier in the year.

As we entered the building and walked down the hall towards my classroom, it finally hit me that my first year of teaching was almost over. Looking at the clock, there were only a few minutes left. The kids began gathering their backpacks and notebooks and started dancing around the room in celebration.

"Okay, line up, everyone," I told them. A few of them wandered towards the door. Most of them didn't even hear me. It was just like the first day when I tried to get their attention, a déjà vu moment. "Ladies and gentlemen," I said a little louder. "If you'd like to start your summer vacation...*on time*, then line up by the door, please." The smile on my face made it clear that I wasn't irritated or mad. This time, they all shuffled toward the door. "Before you leave, I'd like to wish you all a great summer vacation. Don't be strangers," I said. As they walked past, I stuck out my hand and gave each student a hearty handshake. In the back of my head, I wondered what I would be doing at this moment had I not run into Tim Fritz at Glen's back in December. I shuddered at the thought. An image of me chasing them out of the room with a yardstick crept in for a second. I smiled, reached out my hand, looked each kid in the eye, and said, "Have a good summer." It may not seem like much, but I meant every word.

Epilogue

As the summer months melted away, I had a good feeling about the next school year. Standing on the sidewalk during our annual Town & Country Days while waiting for the parade to begin, I felt a quiet calm wash over me. The high school marching band could be heard in the distance, along with the sirens of police cars and fire trucks and the endless chatter of anticipation. I was looking forward to seeing my dad walking with the Sons of Encouragement, handing out fliers for their annual chicken barbeque.

Off to the east, away from the noise, stood the old grain elevator. I'd driven by it thousands of times on my way into town over the last two and a half decades. Looking off in the distance, thinking about the last year of my life, I couldn't help but smile inside. Earlier that day, I had seen a few students from last year. A couple of them actually said "Hello" when they saw me. I was just thankful no one tried to attack me.

As the anticipation of the parade built up inside me, I stopped for a moment to be thankful for all I had. A new love interest. The beginning of a better relationship with my parents. A trusted friend who saw not what I was, but what I was capable of becoming. Most of all, I was thankful for the opportunity to take what I'd learned and start applying it to the people around me. Standing there waiting for the endless line of parade participants to go by, I allowed the peace that came from being content to permeate my entire being.

A Word from the Author

As an undergraduate taking education classes at Central Michigan University, I thought I had everything about teaching figured out. The fact that I actually had no experience had little, if any, influence on the haughty opinion I had of my talents. Of course, I never told anyone how great I thought I was. That would have been arrogant. I may have acted humble on the outside, but inside was a different story. Not long into my student teaching, reality came knocking. Through a series of disappointments and unmet expectations, my vision of what "*could be*" melted into "*What the heck happened?*" My naïve over-confidence was swept away and replaced by varying degrees of disappointment and anxiety.

My vision of enriching children's lives, being a well-respected individual, and flat out having fun with kids had been attacked by thirty students with flame-throwers. At the end of the day, there was nothing left but a thin trail of smoke from my burnt self-image gliding gently away on a late autumn breeze. Waking up every morning with a knotted stomach overflowing with angst had a way of causing me to come to my senses and bring life back to basics. Standing in front of a bunch of kids who would love nothing more than to see me stumble through a lesson by putting out small fires (blurting out, making all sorts of strange noises, kicking each other under the desk, writing notes... you name it!) was quite possibly the best part of their day. "Why is your face so red?" became a question hurled my way many times. *Because you kids are driving me nuts!! That's why!!!* However, in teaching, like many other jobs, the art of biting one's tongue is a most essential talent. Teachers can never really tell it like it is to the people who need to hear it. (*Your child is really getting on my nerves! Would it be possible to keep him home for a few days so I can try to accomplish something?*) We'd love to say what's on our minds once in a while, but keeping our jobs is a lot more important. (On that note, I would suggest staying out of the teachers' lounge if you happen to be a guest at your child's school. It is only there that teachers can freely express themselves. Yes, there are those who seem do it a lot more than others, but even the popular veteran has an occasional need to vent.)

Like a lot of people, I am rarely ready to listen until my emotions are rubbed raw, right down to the little nubbins. It is similar to that feeling one gets while dreaming of being in church or school in only one's underwear. Equal parts shame and embarrassment. Life has its way, sometimes, of taking us down a peg or two.

Fortunately, God put people in my path at just the right time—when I was finally ready to listen. When I'd finally reached the end of my wits, there were people there to listen, to offer insight, and ultimately be someone who could see something I couldn't: potential.

I don't look for difficult situations and then go full steam ahead. No, I usually try to navigate around them. Never *through* them. But, as I'm sure you're already aware, trials and tribulations occur a lot more frequently than we'd like, and when we find ourselves in the middle of something nasty, it's nice to have someone in our corner, offering encouragement. Someone who knows not only *what* to say but *when* and *how* to say it.

Whether it be in a career or life in general, it's kind of nice to have someone walk beside us. Someone who sees what we are capable of and, despite our flaws, makes us feel valued and shares their wisdom in small, bite-size pieces. As the wise King Solomon said in the book of Proverbs, "Plans fail for lack of counsel, but with many advisors they succeed." In other words, don't go it alone.

Acknowledgements

A heartfelt "thank you" to the following:

My Heavenly Father—Your constant pursuit of a wandering drifter is too meaningful for words.

Jacinda—Thanks for believing in me and letting me dream. I couldn't have done it without you!

Tim—For sharing your wisdom and helping me understand that everyone has a story.

Fritz—You helped me recognize the importance of good communication through stories of your own.

Mom and Dad—The sacrifices you made on my behalf are still appreciated. (Mom, thanks too for not sending me to the "nut house" when I was younger, even though you threatened several times.)

Ma Hovey and Nellie—Thank you for praying.

Marcia—Your honest feedback was most appreciated.

Dan and Chris—Fellow Lion-Chasers... thanks for walking alongside.

Chief Little-Big-Gut, Roberto Bob, Rosebud, Muy Pequeño, and Tooty-Fruity— Five reasons to smile.

And of course, to the small towns scattered through the heartland that look at change and progress... and need some time to think about it.

For more information about
Scott Bitely
&
Simmer Down, Mr. C
please visit:

scottbitely.com
www.facebook.com/SimmerDownMrC

....

For more information about
AMBASSADOR INTERNATIONAL
please visit:

www.ambassador-international.com
@AmbassadorIntl
www.facebook.com/AmbassadorIntl